STREET KINGS

Lock Down Publications and Ca$h Presents
Street Kings
A Novel by *Hood Rich*

Street Kings

Lock Down Publications
P.O. Box 870494
Mesquite, Tx 75187

Visit our website @
www.lockdownpublications.com

Copyright 2019 Street Kings

First Edition April 2019
Printed in the United States of America

This is a work of fiction. Names, characters, places, and incidents either are products of the author's imagination or are used fictitiously. Any similarity to actual events or locales or persons, living or dead, is entirely coincidental.

Lock Down Publications
Like our page on Facebook: Lock Down Publications @
www.facebook.com/lockdownpublications.ldp
Cover design and layout by: **Dynasty Cover Me**
Book interior design by: **Shawn Walker**
Edited by: **Jill Alicea**

Stay Connected with Us!

Text **LOCKDOWN** to 22828 to stay up-to-date with new releases, sneak peaks, contests and more…

Thank you.

Submission Guideline

Submit the first three chapters of your completed manuscript to ldpsubmissions@gmail.com, subject line: Your book's title. The manuscript must be in a .doc file and sent as an attachment. Document should be in Times New Roman, double spaced and in size 12 font. Also, provide your synopsis and full contact information. If sending multiple submissions, they must each be in a separate email.

Have a story but no way to send it electronically? You can still submit to LDP/Ca$h Presents. Send in the first three chapters, written or typed, of your completed manuscript to:

LDP: Submissions Dept
Po Box 870494
Mesquite, Tx 75187

DO NOT send original manuscript. Must be a duplicate.

Provide your synopsis and a cover letter containing your full contact information.

Thanks for considering LDP and Ca$h Presents.

Hood Rich

Chapter 1

"I still don't understand why you won't allow me to ask your father for the rent money this month. It's not like he doesn't have it," Sondra said before placing a plate of fried chicken, white rice, pinto beans, and cornbread in front of her only son, Noodles.

Noodles looked the plate of food over and sighed in defeat. Every month he and Sondra found themselves in a tough place when it came time to pay the rent. Noodles was eighteen years old, fresh out of high school, and in need of employment. He'd put in a host of applications all over the city of Los Angeles as soon as he graduated from school, but had not been contacted yet. During the school year he was able to obtain employment from the principal doing odd jobs around the school building that usually consisted of cleaning and organizing. Now that the school year was over, he was in desperate need of cash so that he could help his mother with the numerous bills that plagued their household every month.

Noodles shook his head, and as tantalizing as the plate of food looked before him, he pushed it away. The light shone off of the deep wave pattern atop his head. His midnight-dark skin glistened. His eyelids were pulled tight, slanted. He'd inherited them from his mother, Sondra, who was full-blooded Jamaican. He stood 5'10" tall. His body frame was muscular, as if he'd been in athletics his entire life. "I just don't like you asking that nigga for nothing. Not after everything that he did to you. Not after everything that he did to Cheyenne." Cheyenne was his older sister by two years. When it came to his heart, she was second in place, right after his mother.

Sondra smiled weakly and sat across from him. A big roach crawled across the table with an egg hanging partway out of its ass. She allowed it to get partway to her before she knocked it to the floor. She stood up and stepped on it with her house shoe. She was tired of living in the Crenshaw Projects. She prayed for better days and safer nights. But life had been cruel to her. She'd given up a huge chunk of her life for Bronco. Bronco was Noddle's father, or as she liked to refer to him, his sperm donor. They'd left the island of Jamaica together in 2001 just before Noodles was born. They'd not been in the United States more than a year before Bronco was engaged to an Italian woman. Six months later he would marry her, and she would bear his seed. Life had been unkind for a long time, Sondra thought.

"Well, as far as I'm concerned, your father owes us. He's filthy rich, and he's living the good life. There is no reason we should be in the projects struggling the way we are. On top of that, it's not just the rent this month that I have to worry about. It's the rent, the car note, and cable. It's rough, baby. Altogether we're looking at nearly twelve hundred dollars. Where the hell are we going to get that kind of cash from if we don't ask your father?" Sondra questioned, weighing her options in her mind. She knew that she and her son were all alone. They had other relatives, but the majority of them were back on the island, and they were unreliable. The only person she knew that she could depend on for the financial assistance was Bronco. Of course, she also knew what would be expected of her sexually, but it seemed that that came along with the territory. She always felt highly repulsed afterward, but a woman had to do what she had to do. She'd convinced herself that sleeping with Bronco was just a means of survival, that because he was her son's father, it wasn't a form of prostitution.

"What would you have to do for that nigga if he gave you twelve hunnit dollars, Mama? Huh? My pops selfish as hell and I know he ain't about to give you shit fa free, so what's really good?" Noodles asked with his nostrils flared. He hated the thought of his mother being in a financially vulnerable position. Hated that he couldn't step up to the plate the way that he was supposed to. It made him feel worthless. Inadequate. Pussy. His mother was his heart and soul. He wanted to give her the world and everything that she wanted from out of it.

Sondra lowered her head. "I don't want to talk about that, baby. In fact, why don't we change the subject? Don't worry your heart. I'll figure out our financial situation. You know I will."

He slammed his hand on the table. The fork shot into the air and fell on the floor. "No you won't! That's my job! I'm supposed to take care of you. You're my mother. We don't need that nigga fa shit! Fuck him!" Noodles snapped. He stood up with his chest heaving up and down. His vision was cloudy from the coursing of his anger.

"Noodles, your mouth! I've told you about your mouth," Sondra returned. She hated her son's filthy language whenever he got upset, but at the same time, she admired the passion he held in his heart for her. He and Cheyenne were all that she had, and she could clearly tell that Noodles was insane about her all across the board.

He came around the table and pulled her to him. He held her and kissed her forehead. His brown eyes gazed into hers. "On everythang I love, I'm not coming back into this house tonight until I got that twelve hunnit for you. You don't need to depend on no nigga but me. Son or no son, you are my Queen. If we were back home in Jamaica, and my father was not present, it would be my responsibility to make sure that our bills were paid and our household was in order. It's in my blood, Mama. You hear me?" He hugged her tighter to himself. He was crazy about his Queen, a woman that had sacrificed so much for his sister and himself.

Sondra could feel his solid muscles trapping her. Even though she knew that he was a man now, she couldn't help but to imagine him as a five-year-old boy. Her boy. Even back then, he was extremely protective of her. She didn't want to argue with Noodles. He was a hot head, especially when it came to her. If he said that he was going to figure things out, she was sure that he was. "Baby, I love you, and I don't know what you're about to do, but all I can ask is that you be careful. I need you. Do you hear me?" She felt herself becoming emotional over her young Prince. She wished that she had enough strength within herself to detour him from whatever he was thinking, but she understood that he was headstrong. Determined. She could only pray for his safety and wellbeing. Pray that he returned to her before morning.

"I need you too, Mama." He kissed her warm forehead again and hugged her. I'll be home later. Don't wait up."

"Noodles, can you at least eat first? Please, baby?"

He shook his head. "N'all. I'll eat when I get this money for you. I don't deserve to eat until then."

***

Noodles had a right hand man by the name of Filipino. He was the same height as Noodles. Light-skinned with Asian eyes. He was Filipino and Black. He and Noodles had been best friends ever since they were in the seventh grade, and had fought three times over the fact that Noodles had been caught during lunch time in the janitor's closet at their school with Filipino's sister, who was one grade higher than the two boys. Fancii and Noodles had been together ever since, and eventually, Filipino made his peace with their relationship.

Filipino pulled up beside Noodles, who was waiting on the side of the curb in front of his project apartment. It was nine o'clock at night. Hot and humid. The mosquitoes were biting, and Noodles had sweat rolling down his back. He pulled open the door to the 1987 Chevy Caprice and got in. The air conditioner felt like a breath of fresh air. It soothed the torture from the overpowering heat.

"What up, fool?" Filipino asked, handing him a blunt that was rolled so fat that it looked like a brown marker.

"Shit." Noodles took the blunt and pulled off of it. "The goal is twelve hundred before sunrise. My mother got all kinds of bills that's fucking us over. I gotta come through for her or my dead beat-ass father gon' be able to get between her thighs and make her earn the money, if you get by drift? I ain't having that." He took three big pulls from the cigar and inhaled the smoke deeply.

"Yeah, I feel that. Huh." He handed Noodles a Thirty Eight Special. Six shots. "That's you right there. Trust me, you gon' need it. Did you grab a mask?"

Noodles exhaled a cloud of smoke. He pulled a pair of Cheyenne's altered stockings from his waistband. "Yeah, I'm good to go, bruh. Let's get it in. What's going down again?"

Filipino pulled out of the project parking lot. He reached under his seat and placed an Uzi on his lap. The clip hung out of it like a table leg. "Yo, it seem like both of our families are hurting, kid. That's fucked up." He took

11

the blunt back from Noodles. "We gon' hit these li'l niggas' weed spot over here on Normandy. A li'l young nigga named Felix. He been pushing that bag for his brother that just got knocked a couple weeks ago for a body. Rumor is that he holding about five pounds of that Hawaiian Punch Loud from Maui. I know he gotta have a nice amount of cash in that sucker too. We just gon' hit his ass and be on our way. You feel me?" He scanned the streets as he drove with a mug on his face. There was a teardrop under his left eye. Filipino had committed his first murder at the age of twelve and had been knocking heads off ever since then. His temper was just as lethal as Noodles's, and yet somehow, the pair clicked.

Noodles felt the high discover him. His eyes sunk. His mind turned to the possession of money by any means. There was no way that he could face his mother if he couldn't come up with the twelve hundred dollars that was needed to assist her with the bills. Ever since Donald Trump had forced I.C.E. to turn up the heat on all illegal aliens, his mother had not been able to work at various jobs without the fear of being detained by authorities, being an illegal alien herself. This made it extremely hard. But she was his queen. It was his job to figure out their situation. At least, it was how he strongly felt. "Felix about to go down tonight, Filipino. I can't keep seeing my mother struggle, man. That's my heart. I'm her only protection. Her stability."

Filipino pulled his nose. "We eat off the same plate, Cuz. If your people starving, then I'm starving."

"And vice versa." Noodles made sure his feelings were known.

"Let's handle our bidness. We should be in and out in two minutes." He pulled off of the busy intersection and turned down Western. They rode it for a few blocks until they came upon Normandy. Once there, it seemed that all of the street lights were shot out. The block was completely dark. It gave Noodles an eerie feeling. His attention went on high alert.

Filipino pulled into a driveway two houses over from the spot that Felix sold loud out of. The house was abandoned. There were green boards all over the windows. Filipino cut the engine and pulled a mask over his face. Cocked his Uzi. "Let's handle this shit, Cuz." He opened the driver's door. The interior light flipped on.

Noodles jumped out of the car with his Thirty Eight Special cocked. He held it at his side. The weed had him feeling breezy. He was ready for action and everything that came along with it. He jogged on the side of the abandoned house behind Filipino. The gangway was small. A bunch of small rocks were all over the concrete. When they made it to the alley, they continued to jog down it until they came to the backyard of Felix's spot. Filipino stopped in his tracks and faced Noodles. "Check this out, Cuz. I ain't looking to make this no murder scene, but then again, it is what it is. Yo' family starving. My family starving. I'm tired of this shit, Noodles. After we hit this lick, something has to give. It just has to." He crouched down and eased to the back door with Noodles in tow.

Noodles stepped to the back door and placed his Thirty Eight in the small of his back. Filipino nodded. Noodles knocked on the back door three times and waited for a response. The sounds of crickets resonated somewhere in the vicinity. The humidity tapered off only enough to provide a small sense of relief. The backyard was so dark that Noodles couldn't see Filipino as he knelt beside him.

"Say, Cuz, who is it?" came a voice from the other side of the door.

"Say, bruh, what's up with that good-good?" Noodles asked.

Felix stepped to the back of the door and placed his ear to it. "What you tryna get?"

"I got fifty. But it gotta be that same Maui from earlier," Noodles said, holding his strap shoulder high.

Felix laughed. "Oh, it most definitely is." He took the two by four off of the door and unlocked it.

Before he could open it the entire way, Noodle raised his foot and kicked it as hard as he could. The door swung inward and crushed Felix's nose. Blood poured out of it and down to his top lip. He flew backward onto the steps. "What the fuck, man?"

Noodles rushed inside and grabbed him by the throat. He placed the heater to his forehead. "Check this out, homie, we know what you rocking in here. Let's not play no fucking games. We need that Maui, and every lick of cash in the spot. If that don't happen, it's gon' be a muthafuckin' problem. You feel me?"

Felix swallowed his spit. His eyes were bucked wide open. "You don't know who you fuckin wit', Cuz. This some shit you don't wanna do. Trust me on that," Felix mustered.

Filipino stepped in from outside. He brushed past them and into the house with his Uzi leading the way. "If he ain't on shit, bake his ass. Either way, we ain't leaving this spot until we got everything that we came for. Dead man can't tell no tales no way."

Noodles nodded and lowered his eyes. "Yeah, you right about that. You wanna play games, huh? A'ight den, let's play games." He forced the barrel into Felix's eye so hard that the man began to scream. "Where that stash at, nigga? Huh? Where that stash at?" He pressed harder until the barrel was literally so deep within the socket that Felix's right eyeball popped.

"Argh! Muthafucka! Son of a-." He kicked his legs in the air. "Okay. Okay. I'll tell y'all where everything at! Muthafucka, just get that shit out of my eye!" he hollered, shaking, with blood running down the side of his face.

Noodles smiled under his mask. "That's what I wanna hear, nigga. Make this shit lighter on yourself." He yanked him up. "Get yo' punk ass up."

Hood Rich

Chapter 2

Mills peeked down the hallway of the Bel-Air mansion. He waited until Eliza got close enough to the opening of his doorway before he pulled her inside and closed the door behind.

She yelped and tried to push him off of her. "No, stop, Mills. Your father is going to fire me if he catches me in your room. I just got this job. I can't lose it," she whispered, trying to fight him off.

Mills forced her against the door and yanked her tight Burberry skirt above her waist, revealing her blue lace panties underneath. He kissed her tanned neck after brushing her blond hair aside. His thick lips sucked along the vein there. "I got you this job, Eliza. What, you think I got you the job of being my pop's accountant so I couldn't have access to this body? Yeah, right." He sucked her neck again, this time dragging his teeth across her skin.

Chills traveled up and down Eliza's spine. Once again she tried to push Mills off of her. He was her ex. They had dated very briefly, three months, before she caught him and her best friend in the bed together on her birthday. Ever since then she'd hated his guts. To make amends, he'd helped her get the job of being his father Bronco's personal accountant. She hadn't been on the job for two weeks. In the time that she had, Mills made it his business to be at her every chance that he got.

He slipped his hand into her panties and rubbed her bald, fresh Brazilian-waxed pussy lips. When his middle finger dared to slip inside of her, she moaned. Her back arched. Her blue eyes rolled into the back of her head. "Stop, Mills. Please. Get that out of there."

Mills pulled his finger out and sucked it into his mouth. "Damn, that sugar taste good. Get yo' ass down there. Hurry up." He took a step back and dropped his pants. He pulled his dick out of his pants and stroked it. "Come on, Eliza. Hit this ma'fucka like you used to in school. Come on."

She groaned. She was torn between trying to find a way out of the room and not allowing the sight of his chocolate dick to give her tingles. They had only slept together three times, but each time had been better than the last. It was one of the things she missed about him.

His dominant personality. His ability to control every situation. His lust and hunger for her. All of these things drove her crazy. But at the same time, they annoyed her. She couldn't help but remember how he and Hannah had looked entwined together. He'd been between Hannah's thighs, humping away, when she caught them. The sight of her best friend's ankles on his shoulders was enough to make her scream. Eliza took his piece until her hand and thought about pulling it right off of his body. She squeezed it so hard that Mills groaned in pain. This made her laugh deep within.

Mills grabbed a handful of her hair and made a fist. "Stop playing wit' me m. Hurry up. Because you're right, if my Pops catches you, he's definitely going to fire you. We can't let that happen now, can we?" He smiled handsomely, looking into her blue eyes. She stroked his piece and prepared it for the warm recesses of her mouth.

Eliza jumped when she heard the maid close a door down the hallway. She was sure that it was Bronco looking for her. He'd said that he wanted to take a short power nap. That never lasted for more than an hour or so. She'd spent thirty minutes after he'd announced his decision to take a power nap getting some of his affairs in order on social media. She was on her way to grab her charger when Mills accosted her and pulled her inside of one of the many bedrooms inside of the mansion. Now she found herself on her knees. Life was so strange, she thought.

"Come on, Eliza." Mills was starting to get irritated. He knew that she loved to suck dick. The whole three months they were together, she couldn't get enough of his pipe. Her hand was always wandering into his lap. She just had to see it. She couldn't believe its length and girth. Mills thought that she was just obsessed with black dick. The black men in Bel-Air were few. The majority of the ones that were there were so watered down that they were basically white. In his opinion, it was only himself that had swagger like a brotha from the hood.

Another door slammed. Eliza shivered. *Shit. I better go ahead and get this over with*, she thought. *No sense in avoiding the inevitable.* She took ahold of his piece. She licked her lips and looked up at him. "Hey, this is the last time this is going to happen. You hear me?"

Mills smiled. "Yeah, a'ight, that sounds cool." It was furthest thing from what he was thinking. Her vulnerability was too much of a turn on. He planned on having a great time with her whenever he wanted to. He was in control. He always had to be in control.

Eliza swiped at his dick head with her tongue. This sent chills up and down his spine. She sucked the head into her mouth, twirling her tongue around and round it. She grabbed the base and slid it all the way inside. Then her head was moving back and forth, her lips pursed tightly.

Mills groaned. He closed his eyelids tight. He started to shake as he fucked back and forth into her orifice. When he opened his eyes and saw her blue ones peering into his, he nearly came. Her jaws hollowed in and out. Her blond hair was all over the place. She was gorgeous to him. He couldn't deny that fact. He tightened his grip.

She winced and groaned, sucked faster and faster and added more spit. Her fist pumped his dick in unison with her sucking. She wanted him to cum as fast as possible, wanted to get it over with. The last thing she needed was to get caught giving her boss's son head. This was the type of shit you only saw in pornos, she thought.

"Uhhh," Mills moaned. He fucked her mouth harder. The constant sucking sounds were driving him absolutely crazy. In addition to that, her double-D breasts were starting to work themselves out of her blouse. He could already see a hint of her areolas. Her nipples were hard as steel, and they looked so good to him. In one yank, he pulled down her top. Both breasts spilled out. The pink nipples looked like gumdrops, erect and ready to be sucked.

Eliza felt exposed now. A trickle of her essence leaked out of her sex lips. It was the degrading aspect of it all. The fact that she was on her knees, sucking cock, in her boss's home was starting to ignite a fuse deep within her belly. She squeezed her thighs together as she felt the juices drip down the middle of them. Her hole began to vibrate, yearning to be filled.

Mills reached down and held her breast as he fucked her mouth. He pinched the nipple and came upon the brink of his climax. "Uh, shit, Eliza. I'm about to cum, baby. Shit, I'm about to cum." He humped faster.

She looked up at him and sucked, allowed him to thrust into her mouth. She loved the feel of his big penis invading her the way that it was. *Cum in my mouth*, she thought. *I wanna taste that cream so bad, Mills. Fuck I do*, she screamed inside of her head.

"Uhhh. Mmm," Mills groaned. He came hard, jerking like crazy, his seed spewing into her mouth.

Now Eliza sucked hungrily. She pumped and sucked, squeezed her fist over the base of his tool and milked him, swallowing every drop of him. When she finished, his dick stood harder than she ever remembered.

Mills pulled her up and picked her up into the air. She involuntarily wrapped her legs around him. Her big breasts pressed into his chest. He slammed her against the wall and sucked a gumdrop into his mouth. He licked circles around the areola.

Eliza shivered. She sucked her bottom lip into her mouth and moaned, remembering how hard his dick was below them. She started to imagine what it would feel like to slide down upon it, to feel him stretching her wide open, to see his black pipe going in and out of her snow white box. She shuddered and moaned deep within her throat as his big lips sucked her nipples hard.

Mills tossed her on the bed and got between her thighs. His dick head rested on her sex lips, throbbing like crazy. "You finna give me some of this pussy, Eliza. I'm feening for it," he growled. He sucked her neck and squeezed her big breasts together.

Another hint of juice seeped out if her box and slid into her ass crack. Mills used it to lubricate her bald pussy lips. He opened them and located her clitoris. He ran his thumb in circles around it until she was humping into his hand.

"Get off of me, Mills. Please. You're going to get me into trouble." More humping. She wanted him to take her pussy already. She wondered what he was waiting on.

Mills held her hands out over her head. He sucked her neck and humped into her box. His dick head opened her hot pussy lips, but didn't travel inside. The heat was intox-icating. He took ahold of his pipe and lined it up and got ready to go inside of her furnace. "Open these fuckin' thighs a li'l more, Eliza."

She moaned and arched her back. "No, please don't." But her body screamed, "Please do". It screamed, "Please fuck me now, you son of a bitch."

"Eliza! Eliza! Girl, where are you?" Bronco called, coming down the stairs with a glass of orange juice in his hand.

Eliza perked up. "I gotta go, Mills. Seriously. I gotta go. Get. Off. Of. Me." She pushed him as hard as she could, knocking him off of her body. She jumped up and pulled her skirt down, covering her bald kitten. Then she stuffed her breasts back inside of her top one at a time.

Mills stared at her with his dick in his hand. He pumped it slowly as he watched her get dressed. Sad. Angry. An-noyed, and horny. He had been so close. So, so close.

"This can never happen again, Mills. I mean it. I work for your father now. I can't risk losing my position. This job is going to help me pay my way through college. Well, your dad is. He says that as long as I work for him, he'll continue to foot the bills and that I'll have a spot on his team when he runs for mayor. I intend to have that spot." She smoothed her hands over her breasts. "So no more, Mills. You got me?"

Mills eyes her from head to toe and continued to stroke himself. He had visions of snatching her up and taking the pussy. It would make it so much better. She would have to submit to him then. No way could he ever stop pursuing her. There was just something about her that drove him crazy. But he would tell her whatever she needed to hear for now. "I got you." He got up and slid his boxers up his thighs. He saw that she was on her way out of the room and grabbed her arm and slammed her against the wall. His forehead rested against her. His hand pawed all over her body, snuck under her skirt again and into her panties. "Bitch, as long as you're going to college for free and my Pops is footing the bill for everything, you belong to me. You don't run shit. You are a worker. A pawn. Your job is to keep feeding me the numbers. To learn the financial things of his operations inside and out. If you lose sight of why I put your ass in place, I swear on my mother that I will replace you faster than a flat tire. Now do you get me?" Two fingers slid into her tunnel as his father called out for her again.

She shivered. His dominance was so arousing. It made her weak. She hated and liked him at the same time. Her head spun as she tried her best to collect her thoughts. His fingers ran in and out of her at full speed.

"Do you?"

"Yes. Yes. Yes. I. Do," she moaned.

Hood Rich

Chapter 3

"Nine hundred. One thousand. Eleven hundred. Twelve hundred even. There you go, Mama. You should be able to handle them bills right away." Noodles beamed with pride.

Sondra sat up in bed. She wiped the sleep out of her eyes and gazed over at the clock. It read 3:17 in the morning. Her oscillating fan blew into her face before the breeze disappeared and came back again. It was so humid that her gown was sticking to her back. "Baby, where did you get this money?"

Noodles kissed her cheek and climbed in the bed beside her. He pulled her down to his chest. "Stop playing wit' me, beautiful, you know dang well that ain't yo' bidness. All you worry about is that the bills are paid for another month. I took care of everything just like I was supposed to. I told you I got you, Mama. You're my Queen." He kissed her forehead. There were light traces of sweat there.

"Boy, you better watch yo' mouth and how you talk to me. You be getting real slick at the tongue sometimes, Noodles. Be making me wanna pop you right on those lips," she admitted. She picked yo the money and smiled.

"You don't wanna do that, Mama." He frowned.

She raised her right eyebrow. "Oh, is that so? And why don't I?"

He was silent for a few seconds, and then he tackled her to the bed and began to kiss all over her beautiful face. "Because then I couldn't use them to do this. Gimme some. Gimme some." More kissing. Nearly every portion of her face. Again and again.

Sondra couldn't help but to laugh louder and louder. Her son was always doing the unthinkable. He always making her feel like a kid again. He had this way about helping her to escape the valley of depression that often encompassed her. He was her light in the often dark world. She loved him with all of her heart and soul.

When he stopped, he hugged up with her. He rested his lips against her temple. "Mama, I'm sorry for talking that street talk to you, and for cursing in front of you yesterday. My temper is horrible. Especially when it comes to you. You're my heart. I don't like to imagine you struggling in this world. You deserve the best of the best and it's my job to get it for you." He held her tighter as the fan blew across them and went on its path of cooling down the room as best it could. *I gotta buy my mama an air conditioning unit*, he thought.

Sondra sat up and wiggled out of his embrace. She sighed. "It's not your place to worry about me like this, Noodles. You're my son. I'm supposed to be worried about your welfare and how I'm going to provide for you. Not the other way around." She felt so weak. So powerless. All she wanted to do was work. But I.C.E. wasn't playing any games with illegal aliens, even though Los Angeles was supposed to be a sanctuary city.

Noodles slid out of the bed and punched his hand. "Says who? Who says that my mother is supposed to provide for a grown-ass man? Who?"

"Noodles, your mouth!"

"Nall, screw that. What type of nigga sits around, grown as hell, and lets his mother take care of him? What kind? Huh?"

The covers fell off of Sondra. She adjusted her night gown and cleared her throat. Just when she was about to let him know what she thought about that, he cut back in.

"A bitch nigga. Any nigga that a sit on his monkey ass, and a let his mother, or any female for that matter take care of him need a bullet in his head. You are my Queen. I'm all you got. My father played you like a sucker. Played me like a sucker. We don't need that nigga, or nobody else. It's just me, you, and my sister. I got you, Mama. I'ma buy you a house, move you out of this bogus-ass project. You deserve your own home. Your own car and truck. You ain't supposed to be working when I'm able to go out here and get it. You are my Queen. You hear me?" He was back in the bed and holding her again. His face frowned, heart beating hard in his chest. He couldn't help but to imagine the streets of Los Angeles: the many blocks, the different gangs, the risks, the dangers, the survival that had to supersede everything else. He wanted to conquer it all - not for himself, but for the welfare and stability of his sister and mother.

Sondra laid her head on his shoulder. "I love you, Noodles. The way you care for me is so refreshing. So unbelievable. You are my greatest gift, baby. I just want you to know that."

"Nall, you're mines, Mama. You gave me life. You carried me. You nourished me and fed me from your body. I could never repay you for all that you've done for me. But I'm going to break my neck trying. You are precious." He kissed her forehead again and felt a sense of over-protectiveness come over him. He held her tighter.

Sondra shook her head. She didn't know what to say. Tears formed in the corners of her eyes and sailed down her cheeks. She loved Noodles so much. She didn't understand how he could be so crazy about her. All of their life had been a struggle. They'd lived in one low income place after the next. One dangerous, rundown, drug infested neighborhood after the other. How could Noodles love her in the way that he did when all she'd done was fail him?

"Thank you for saying that, baby. And thank you for making it happen for our family again. You really are my heart's joy." She kissed him and nestled into his arms. "Tell me some more about this house, baby. How many rooms is it going to have?"

Noodles smiled. He allowed for her to lay back on his chest as he held her protectively. "It's going to be two levels – well, three if you factor in the attic. No less than four bedrooms and two baths, just like you always wanted."

"Will it have a two car garage? You know, one for my car, and the other for my truck that we're going to get one day?"

"Of course. And it'll be a brick home. With a fireplace, and a pool in the backyard," Noodles assured her.

"Yeah, and to the right will be a nice area for my garden. I want to grow my own vegetables. All organic. And I'll set up my table, and get me a bottle of wine to drink back there while I just relax and listen to the Isley Brothers serenade me. Then the insides will be fully furnished with white carpet, and a kitchen that I'll make you and your sister some of the greatest meals out of. I'll..."

Noodles yawned as he listened to her go on and on. The more she talked, the more determined her became to get her out of the projects and into her own home. She deserved it, he felt. And in his heart, he knew that he had to be the one to get it for her. He had to protect and bless his Queen.

***

Two days later, Filipino pulled into Crenshaw's project parking lot, just as Noodles was bringing the garbage out to the dumpster on a bright and sunny afternoon. He had Fancii in the driver's seat. When she saw Noodles, she jumped out of the Chevy and ran over to him, her long natural hair flowing behind her.

Noodles put the garbage on the ground and opened his arms. They embraced. Fancii smelled sweet, like vanilla perfume. He hugged her and brushed her hair out of her face. "Hey baby, what are you doing here?" he asked, wondering why she hadn't texted him first.

Fancii smiled and sucked on her bottom lip nervously. "I booked my first modeling gig, Noodles. I'm going to be modeling for Nine West. If this goes well, my agent says that my career could take off. Could you imagine that? Do you know where this could take us?" She was excited. She wrapped her arms around his neck again and screeched.

He held her by the waist, impressed. "Baby, that is amazing. I'm so proud of you. I knew you could do it. I just knew you could." Then they were making out. His hands traveled all over her ample backside, cuffing the hefty cheeks back there. She wore a pair of tight-fitting Jordache jeans that hugged her curves in a righteous manner. Fancii was 5'8" tall, slim thick, with light brown eyes and long hair that stopped at her waist. She was mixed with Filipino and Black just like her brother, Filipino. She was gorgeous in every sense of the word. Noodles was crazy about her because she was ambitious, goal-oriented, a dreamer and go-getter. She aspired to be something great, and was trying desperately to master her destiny.

"Thank you, baby. You already know that wherever this journey takes me that I want you right beside me at all times. Oh...I love you so much, Noodles." She hugged him again.

Filipino walked over to the pair with a big blunt in his mouth. "Alright. Alright. Break it up. I get it, you two are in love. Please save all of this shit for the bedroom," he cracked.

Fancii turned around and stood in front of Noodles. She forced him to wrap his arms around her waist. "Well, if you don't wanna see me and my man celebrate my success and our love for each other, it's best that you turn your head. I love him and he loves me, and that's just the way it is." She rolled her eyes and turned back to face Noodles. "Ain't that right, baby?"

Noodles looked into her eyes, mesmerized by her beauty. "Hell yeah, that's right. You my baby. Cuz already know that." He looked over her shoulder into Filipino's face.

Filipino looked at the ground, angry. "Well, whenever you two lovers can pry your hands away from each other, I need to holler at you, Noodles, about a nice amount of cash."

Fancii smacked her lips and scoffed. "Whatever. I wanna tell Mom the good news anyway. Is she in the house, Noodles?" she asked, speaking in terms of Sondra.

Noodles nodded. "Yeah, she in there. She was just talking about you too, baby. Go on in there and let me holler at bruh for a minute."

She nodded. "That's cool, but what do you say we go out for dinner after I come back from my gig? You know, as a nice celebration. That's cool?" She kissed his lips ever so tenderly. Her tongue traced the bottom, and then the top one.

Noodles felt his piece hardening. He pulled her more firmly to himself. He imagined how tight her pussy felt around his pipe and had visions of bending her over the bed in his room and killing that cat from the back. Fancii had some of the best pussy he'd ever had in his life. "That sound like a master plan, baby. You can hold me to it."

She laughed and humped forward, feeling his penis harden down his thigh. "I bet I can. Alright then, see you in a minute, baby." She rolled her eyes at Filipino and jogged up the walkway toward Sondra's apartment.

Filipino shook his head and looked up to Noodles. "Damn, nigga, you gotta be all over her while I'm right here?" He blew a cloud of smoke to the sky.

"Nigga, I don't be saying shit when you be all over Cassie," Noodles snapped.

"Yeah, but Cassie ain't your sister. You grabbing her ass and shit. Damn, nigga. Now that shit burnt into my brain." He shook his head as hard as he could.

"Stop being so fuckin' dramatic. That's my baby. I love her. It is what it is. Deal wit' it." Noodles glanced around the projects. "What's good wit' this money?"

There were a bunch of children out. Some were chasing each other back and forth. A group of girls were taking turns jumping Double Dutch. They sang nursery rhymes as they stood in the sideline, waiting their turn. In the middle if the parking lot were nineteen boys playing two hands touch football. A group of hustlers sold their narcotics on one end of the parking lot while on the other, a few people were washing their cars, getting them prepared to cruise through the streets of Los Angeles. It was a typical start to the day, another summer in L.A.

"I just got word from that fool Twan that he wanna meet up with us. He say he got a few moves for us to bust. Moves that could put some serious dough in our pockets. I wanna link up with him and see what he talking about."

Noodles ran a list of dudes named Twan through his mental Rolodex until he settled on the one that he was sure

Filipino was speaking on. "You talking about that crazy nigga that be over on Normandy?"

Filipino nodded his head. "Bingo. I wanna get up with him and get some of that fast money. He be having licks lined up all over L.A."

"Yeah, well, I heard he dropped dime in a few niggas from Oakland, and they put a fifty thousand dollar price tag on his head."

Filipino waved that off. "Man, that's just a fuckin' rumor. He don't even get down like that. You know how ma'fuckas be trying to assassinate a nigga's character because they jealous. This city full of that shit."

"Yeah, well, when we supposed to be hollering at this fool?" Noodles picked up the bag and placed it inside of the garbage.

Filipino pulled a pair of Lakers tickets out of his pocket. "Tonight. We four rows from the floor. LeBron gon' be in the house, and Durant. That ma'fucka gon' be lit. I say we go out and see what's good."

Noodles stood in the sunlight and rubbed his chin. "Do that fool be talking some major numbers?"

Filipino smiled. The sun reflected off of his forehead. "I wouldn't be trying to fuck wit' him if he wasn't."

Noodles thought about the bills that would resurface next month and thought it was in his best interest to get a jump start on them. He didn't want his mother worrying about them. The less she worried, the better. He took a deep breath and inhaled the fresh air of Los Angeles. He could smell one of his neighbors barbecuing. "A'ight, set that shit up. This nigga better be talking some straight numbers too."

Filipino smiled. "He will. We already established all of that."

Chapter 4

Mills dropped the top on his 2020 black on black Porsche with the all-red leather seats. He adjusted the steering wheel and waited for Kelly to ease into the passenger's seat. He started the track by Travis Scott, "Tear the Club Up", and beeped the horn again.

Kelly walked out of the house, still trying to find the hole in her ear for her earring. "Jesus Christ, Mills, stop blowing that damn horn. I'm walking as fast as I can." Her tight, red Prada dress clung to her curves. It made it slightly difficult to walk, along with the red-bottomed heels. She took her place in the car beside her brother, then finally fixed the earring into her hole.

Mills was honey-colored, 5'11" tall. He had brown eyes and an athletic build, with a low Mohawk-style haircut that had natural curls.

Kelly was full-blooded Italian with green eyes and long brunette hair. She stood at 5'6" tall. She had a nice figure that got her lots of cat calls from white and black men. She was two years older than Mills, and she loved her brother more than anyone else in the world. She threw her hair over her shoulders and goaded him. "Why do you always do that?"

"Do what?" Mills asked, starting the ignition and backing out of the long driveway, which led to a big metal gate. Once there he punched in a series of digital numbers, and the gate buzzed and slowly began to open. "Do what?"

"You always take a million years to get ready. I wait patiently for you while you run back and forth like a chicken with your head cut off. I stay out of the way. But then when it's my turn to get dressed, you rush out of the house and to the car. Every fucking five minutes you're blowing the horn. It drives me nuts. Uhhh!" She wanted to choke him.

Mills laughed and looked over at her. "You'll be alright. Besides, you look good. You ain't need to spend no more time getting yourself together."

Kelly sucked her teeth and fixed her boobs inside of her bra to make sure they were sitting up the right way. In doing so, she accidentally flashed Mills more than once.

"Hey. Damn, sis. Put them jokers away." He nearly crashed into the curb heading past the gates of their parent's estate.

"Well, enjoy the show, because you rushed me. I have to make sure that I look absolutely perfect for this event. There are going to be a bunch of agents and model scouts there. I want to impress everybody in the room. I'm shooting for a *Vogue* spread."

Mills smiled. "Yeah, and I'm shooting to lock down more than a few of these models that are going to be here. I need some more pretty faces at my club. If I can knock a few of these model broads, man, I can take Club Flawless to the next level," Mills said out loud, already envisioning the possibilities for his strip club. He would be eighteen in a few months, and his father promised to turn over the club to him on his birthday. He couldn't wait. He'd been putting females in place inside of it already and running the night-by-night operations at his father's behest.

"You're always thinking about you, Mills. For once, can you think about somebody else? Huh, can you?" Kelly asked, fixing her red Kylie Jenner lipstick in the mirror. She added a sheen of gloss and blew a kiss at her reflection. "This night is supposed to be all about me." She ran her tongue across her teeth.

Mills kept on driving. "Sis, if I don't think about me, then who will?"

She rolled her eyes. "Mills, you think about yourself a little bit too much. Why don't you give somebody else a chance to think about you?" She squeezed her breasts together, and readjusted them. "I think I went too big. These puppies might be the reason I'm never able to land a *Vogue* spot. Damn."

Mills felt some type of way about the comment his sister had made about him. He felt ready to blow. Kelly was always saying comments that bruised his ego. He tried his best to not let on how much she irked his nerves at times. Instead of snapping out at her, he decided to take another approach. After all, if he stood any chance of hooking up with a bunch of models, Kelly would be essential. She had a knack of pulling dames for him - a knack that he needed. "Sis, you know what? Today is about you. I'm sorry, and hey, I know you're going to land a *Vogue* booking. You're absolutely gorgeous. *Vogue* would be so lucky as to have such a model to grace their pages."

Kelly's neck nearly snapped. She shot a stare at him. Their eyes peered into one another's. "What did you say?" she asked in utter disbelief.

"You heard me." He placed his hand on her knee.

She melted. "That's why I love you, Mills. I know you've always got my back. I just hope you know that I got yours as well."

He smiled. "I know you do, sis. It's us against the world."

***

Later that night, Mills caroused the crowd of beautiful women as they sipped on glasses of champagne, and talked a lot about the day's events. The models ranged from medium height to tall, very slim, to plus-sized. They came in all colors. Ninety percent of them were insanely gorgeous to him. Every time his eyes settled on one, he found another one that was ten times more beautiful. He felt like he'd died and gone to heaven. The array of scents in the room was something else that was driving him mad. He knew that if he could get two of them alone he could turn them on to some quality coke, and a proposition that would make them forget about the modeling world.

Kelly came across the room holding the hand of an exotic beauty. Mills couldn't take his eyes off of her. She had golden-colored skin and Asian eyes. As she got closer, he could make out light freckles on her face. He felt breathless.

"Mills. Hey, where the hell have you been? I was looking all over for you," Kelly asked.

Mills stepped to his sister, but he couldn't take his eyes off of Fancii. "Sis, who is this?"

Fancii smiled and batted her eyelashes. She'd heard about the Banks family and was familiar with Kelly's stepfather. He was currently an alderman in the city of Los Angeles. He'd spoke numerous times at her school and spearheaded the Stop the Violence movement in 2019. The rundown duplex that she and her family stayed inside was in his district. There were rumors that Bronco Banks was set to run for mayor of the city and had a nice shot of obtaining the seat. If that was so, her being entwined within the family would be a benefit. She didn't know just how yet, but she foresaw it being beneficial for the future.

Kelly laughed. He could tell that she was slightly tipsy. Her eyes were low and red. "This is my friend Fancii. Isn't she gorgeous?"

Mills nodded as he looked Fancii in her pretty eyes. "Yeah. Gorgeous is an understatement. You are flawless, baby." He took her hand and kissed the back of it. "My name is Mills Banks. Son of Bronco Banks."

Fancii smiled. "I know who you are. Your sister talks about you all the time. Also, I am familiar with your father's work. I appreciate his efforts to restore the Crenshaw community."

Mills nodded. He didn't know what the hell she was talking about. "Well, it was my idea. I've always looked at Crenshaw as being a more intricate part of Los Angeles. I feel that if we can restore it, then the rest of the leaders, and our people, will see the efforts there and take heed to their own communities. I drive through it often and try to imagine what the area is to become. That community matters to me, especially the people there." Mills had never been to Crenshaw a day in his life, and never planned on going. It was extremely dangerous. He didn't see the point – unless, of course, it was where Fancii stayed. He'd make that journey for her - at least until he got the goods, anyway.

"Wow, that's pretty cool," Fancii replied. She looked him up and down, and found him crazily handsome with his honey skin, foreign features, muscular body, and deep voice. His cologne was intoxicating as well. She had to snap out of it and remember that she belonged to Noodles. She wished that he could have accompanied her to the get together. If there was one thing about their relationship that she wished they could build up on, it was his presence and support of her. She wanted him to think outside of the hood some times. It was imperative.

"Fancii, what are you doing after this little soiree?" Mills asked, eyeing her physique. No doubt, she was bad to him in every sense of the word.

Fancii laughed. "You don't waste no time, do you?"

"Not when I'm standing in front of the most beautiful woman in the world," he flirted, and in that moment, he honestly felt like she was. He wondered if she tasted as good as she looked.

"Hey." Kelly felt offended.

Fancii laughed and enjoyed the compliment. Then she felt guilty because of the thought of Noodles. She had to get out of there. Filipino would be out front to pick her up as soon as she called him. "Well, actually, I was about to call my brother so he could pick me up."

"Nonsense." Mills stepped forward and took hold of her hand again. "I got a 2020 Porsche parked outside, and it has more than enough room for you. In fact, it would be lonely without you."

Fancii giggled. "No, I better not."

"Yeah, because she has a boyfriend, Mills. She talks about him all the time. A rough neck from Crenshaw. You don't want those kinds of problems now, do you?" Kelly teased.

Mills swallowed. Of course he didn't. The last thing he needed was to be involved with some low life street punk. But he had to hold his composure. Stand his ground. "If those problems have anything to do with Fancii here, then I'm all in. I can look at her and tell she's worth the danger." Their eyes met.

Fancii held his gaze for a few seconds, felt a chill go down her spine, and looked away. Why did he have to be so handsome? That fact was killing her. She needed to see Noodles again. The distinguished Mills was picking at her defenses. Something about him intrigued her. His aura piqued her interests in more ways than one.

"If you don't mind, I'll drop you off. I swear it wouldn't be a bother," Mills promised.

Fancii snapped her head back. "You're going to drive a brand new Porsche into Crenshaw? Really?"

"If that's what it's going to take in order for me to get a few more minutes of your time, I sure am," he assured her.

Fancii felt honored. She didn't think there would be any harm in accepting a ride from him. Besides, he was the son of Bronco Banks, the millionaire real estate mogul turned politician. "Okay then. I'll send my brother a text telling him that I found a ride and that I'll be home soon."

One of the casting directors for the CW network tapped Kelly on the shoulder and pulled her to the side to talk business. He was interested in giving her a small part in a script he'd written.

Mills took hold of Fancii's hand. "I swear, I don't care what it takes. Even if it costs me my life. I'm going to get to know you. Wherever you are trying to go in life, I wanna help you get there. You hear me?"

Fancii looked into his eyes and nodded. It felt like there were a million butterflies in her stomach. She couldn't understand the feeling. It was strange. It made her afraid. His penetrating gaze seemed to freeze her in place. Before she could stop herself, the words were rolling off of her tongue. "Yes. I hear you."

Mills stared into her pretty eyes and held her gaze. His thumb brushed back and forth across the soft skin of her hands. "Alright then, as soon as my sister's ready, we'll roll out." He had plans for Fancii. She did something to him. Something that he couldn't quite put his finger on. All he knew for sure was that he had to have her. He would allow nothing to get in his way.

Hood Rich

Chapter 5

Noodles settled into his seat inside of the legendary Staple Center just as the third minute of the first quarter began. Filipino sat beside him. He had a Pepsi, two hot dogs, and a platter of nachos with jalapeño peppers all over them. It looked good to Noodles, and it smelled even better. But the sight of all of the food also pissed him off. He felt that Filipino was getting way too comfortable for a business meeting of sorts. Filipino sipped out of the straw and set his drink beside his foot.

Noodles mugged him. "Bruh, what the fuck is wrong wit' you?"

Filipino dragged his eyes from the game and looked over at Noodles, confused. "What's eating you, bruh?"

"You, nigga. I should have stopped yo' ass from buying all this bullshit. We're supposed to be here to talk business, not eating a whole fuckin' buffet. Not to be comfortable. Not to take shit so lightly. This is strictly about our advancement so we can feed out families more consistently. All this shit you got going on is extra." Noodles mugged the food again and shook his head.

"Yeah, well, whatever, nigga. I ain't ate shit all day. I been meaning to sit still so I could, but I haven't. Well, I'm sitting still now, and I'm finna enjoy this shit. You can stay irritated while I do this." He picked up a hotdog and shoved it into his mouth, bit down on it, and chewed with his mouth wide open.

Noodles felt like punching him right in the nose, but instead he laughed. "You silly, cuz. I feel like hitting you in yo' shit. Straight up." He scanned the crowd and all of the exits that he could see. The arena was packed. There was a sea of fans wearing gold and purple LeBron jerseys.

LeBron was Noodles's favorite basketball player. He rubbernecked to see if he could locate him, and when he did, he nodded to no one in general.

Filipino washed down his hotdogs with the Pepsi. "Say, Noodles, when dude get here, make sure at all times you refer to him as Combo. I don't know why he rocking wit' that name now, but just do it. He made that perfectly clear when we hollered a few hours ago." He shoved a bunch of nachos into his mouth and crushed them with his teeth, closed his eyes, and shook his head. They tasted so good with the jalapeño peppers all over them. Filipino loved spicy foods. It was his weakness.

Noodles watched LeBron dunk the ball so hard it rattled the rim. The stadium went nuts. They jumped to their feet and cheered. "Man, I don't give a fuck what he wants me to call him. Long as he talking about some serious paper, that will be steady. Besides, just 'cause a nigga changes his name don't mean that cats won't know who he is, and I hope it wasn't to evade the feds. They definitely ain't that stupid."

Filipino stuffed the rest of the last hotdog into his mouth and forced a few nachos inside of the small amount of room that was left. He crushed them all at the same time. His jaws were puffed out. "Noodles." More smacking. "Just be cool, man." Crunching. Smacking. Filipino swallowed half of the food and kept chewing. "You got a bad temper." More chewing. Smacking loudly. He swallowed everything and picked up the Pepsi, drained half the soda pop and set it back by his foot. "You know how you are when it comes to other men and them giving you orders, bruh. You hate it. I do too, but for now we need to see what's good with Combo. If he can put us up on some serious cash, we forced to take heed."

Noodles flared his nostrils. He hated the fact that whenever it was time to meet a new connect, Filipino always made it seem like he carried on poorly. That wasn't the case. He just felt he was good at calling bullshit, and he refused to stand for it. "Fuck you, nigga. I don't know what you talking about. If this ma'fucka ain't coming correct, I'm calling that shit. That's just gon' be that. The graveyard is full of send-offs. I ain't gon' be one of them. You can bet that." He mugged the stadium of fans again, searching for faces of enemies. After not locating any, he sat back and pulled his phone out. He saw that there was a text from Fancii telling him that the night had been amazing. She wished he was there, and she would meet him at his mother's place soon. "Bruh, how the fuck Fancii getting home? I thought you was supposed to pick her up?"

Filipino downed the rest of his Pepsi. "N'all, she said she was getting a ride." He shrugged his shoulders. "I'm off the hook."

Noodles was about to question him in regards to who she was getting a ride from when Combo appeared in the aisle. He stood 5'6" tall. He was dark-skinned, with a bald head and goatee. His clothes were all Gucci. He wore a sweater that covered the lower portion of his face with a bunch of gold chains over it. He made his way down the aisle. Noodles and Filipino moved so he could sit in the middle. Four of his security team members filled the seats directly behind the trio.

Combo eased into his spot and sighed. "What's good, fellas? Excuse my tardiness, I had a prior engagement."

Filipino shook up with him. "It's cool, cuz. We get that you're a busy man. This my brother Noodles right here. We do everything together. Noodles, this is Combo."

Noodles shook up with him and sat back in his seat. "Good to finally meet you, homie."

"Likewise," Combo returned. He looked from Filipino to Noodles and smiled under his Gucci sweater. "I can't believe it's you two pretty boy-ass niggas that's been bringing so much terror to the city. Both of y'all got a hell of a resume. Label me impressed."

"Impressed is one way to go. I hope that means you're about to put us up on some serious cash. If not, this here is a waste of time," Noodles said, looking out to the game.

Filipino mugged him. "What my brother means is that it's hard out here. We're trying to link up with you so you can put us up on some real scratch. We been hitting traps for a li'l bit of nothing. One month of rent money and shit like that. We're looking to be stable. Got a lot of people that's eating off of our plates."

Combo nodded. "I hear that. That's why I called you li'l dudes out today. I got some work for you. The jobs will start out small, and will gradually get better. You gotta crawl before you walk. You know how that go."

"Man, I ain't crawled since I Facetimed my first nigga at thirteen years old. Walked right up to his punk ass and boom. Knocked his muthafuckin' head off. Ripped his pockets from his jeans and took my five dollar bill back. It's been on ever since," Noodles bragged. He looked Combo in the eyes. "What type of crawling you talking about doing, cuz?"

Filipino was heated. He prayed that Noodles didn't blow things for them. Out of all of the big timers in the city, Combo was the most plugged. He had his hands in a little bit of everything. They needed to be connected with him. It would be the first step toward them securing their own portion of the streets. "Combo, what do you have in mind?"

Combo sat back and ran his tongue across his teeth. "I'ma have y'all start with a few businesses that need to pay protection fees to the family. It's four of them. If you can get them to agree to pay two thousand apiece each month, I'll give you two a G a piece, and you'll progress to the next stage. Sound like a plan?"

"Sound like some bulky shit to me. That ain't my style, cuz. I ain't finna go bullying some fuckin' business where people are in there trying to make an honest living to support their families. That's fuck shit. If I'ma force somebody to give me their hard earned money, it's gon' be a ma'fucka that can clap back at me. A hustler. A killer like myself. Ain't no bitch in me, and I ain't pulling no bum, low level strong arms. You can come better than that," Noodles said, feeling like he was ready to jump up and say fuck Combo altogether. He imagined his mother running a business and some nigga rushing in with a gun trying to force her to pay him a sum of her hard-earned money every week. He was sure that he would waste that dude and his whole crew of pussies with no remorse.

"Do you know who you talking to, Noodles?" Combo asked, ready to stand up.

Noodles scoffed. "Yeah, I do, but clearly you don't. I don't know what you're used to, but ain't no send-offs over here, Combo. It's clear that you ain't on shit." He stood up. "Let's be out, Filipino."

Filipino stood up. "Noodles, chill. Let's hear him out."

Combo mugged Noodles. He had visions of putting two in the young man's head. He didn't like the utter disregard for his stature. Noodles needed to be taught some respect, he felt, and he would have loved to be the one to teach him. "Both of y'all sit ya asses down. I'm not finished talking yet."

45

Noodles shrugged his shoulders, as the crowd jumped up, cheering. They began to shout, "Defense, defense, defense."

"Look, I don't give a fuck if you're finished talking or not. I already see how you've appraised us. Clearly you think we're less than what I know we are. If you ain't talking no serious cake, then this meeting is over. Period," Noodles warned.

Combo stood up and faced Noodles. "Nigga, I said sit yo' ass down. I'm not finished talking yet, cuz. This my muthafuckin' city. I run those streets, and you muthafuckas gon' do what the fuck I say do. Now sit the fuck down."

Filipino frowned. "Hold on, nigga, you can take some of that bass out of your voice. Ain't no hoes over here."

Combo turned toward him and stepped into is face. "What you say, li'l nigga?"

Noodles felt his heart beating fast. He grabbed Combo by the shoulders and pulled him out of Filipino's face. "Get the fuck out my nigga's face, boy. You ain't on shit. On everythang, you ain't in shit wit' us, cuz."

Combo's men stood up, ready for action. All it would have taken was for him to give them the signal, and they would have attacked both Noodles and Filipino with the intent to cause serious bodily harm.

Combo looked at his shoulder and brushed off the spot where Noodles had touched him. He glared at Noodles. "You just fucked up, homeboy. Ain't no nigga ever laid hands on me without getting his head knocked off."

Noodles balled his fist. "Oh yeah? Well I ain't never been one to fuck up without really fucking up. So let me really fuck up then."

The crowd jumped up and cheered after a monster dunk from LeBron. Noodles cocked back and swung as hard as

46

he could. When his fist slammed into Combo's nose, it broke it on impact. Combo flew back into Filipino's arms. Filipino slung him into the seats, and punched him as hard as he could in the ear canal. Then both friends took off running in opposite directions.

Combo's men stood there stunned. They didn't know what to do. By the time they figured they should pursue the pair, the security staff invaded the aisle they were sitting in. Combo was knocked out on the floor cold with blood rushing out of his nose. The event staff rushed to him to offer help and to obtain medical assistance.

***

Filipino paced back and forth in his basement. He puffed on a big blunt, blowing smoke into the air. He was heated, in disbelief, and irritated. "You do that shit every time, Noodles. Every time we try and link up with somebody, you always get into it with them. It never fails."

Noodles spread the Maui Loud down the center of his split Garcia Vega before twisting it like a professional. He didn't feel like he had done anything wrong. He felt like Combo was in the wrong for thinking they were a bunch of chumps. He got everything that he deserved. Noodles wished it could have been far worse. "Fuck that nigga, Filipino. We don't need him or nobody else. If we gon' provide for our families and make shit happen, we gon' have to do it ourselves. Me and you come from the dirt together. We been figuring shit out on our own together. Fuck Combo. This pussy nigga thought he was about to have us shaking down hardworking people. Mothers. Fathers. In our community, more than likely. Man, I ain't wit' that shit."

Filipino shook his head. He was frustrated. "But shit ain't have to go that far, Noodles. What made you buss him in his shit?" Filipino wanted to know.

Noodles shrugged his shoulders. "He deserved it. It was simple as that."

Filipino mugged Noodles for a long time, and then busted up laughing. He sank to the couch and busted a gut. "Man, you broke his nose, Noodles. There was blood everywhere. You know we gon' have to beef with that nigga, don't you?"

Noodles set fire to his blunt. "He's saying that he runs Los Angeles. That these streets are his. In order to get our piece of the pie, we were going to have to go through him anyway. But I'll tell you what, that one punch felt so muthafuckin' good. I just wish it was a bullet."

Filipino was high as a kite. "Well, before he comes at us, I'ma talk to my cousin Eddie. He was the one that told me not to get involved with Combo. He said that he is trash. A low life."

"Then why the fuck was you trying to?" Noodles snapped. He took a huge puff from the Maui and inhaled. He already felt like he was floating on air.

Filipino set his blunt in the ashtray. "Because he wasn't trying to fuck wit' us. He says that we're not old enough. That we're not ready for his level of involvement in the Game. That pissed me off, so I wanted us to go against the grain. I'm tired of everybody underestimating us, Noodles. They all act like we're beneath them. It pisses me off. I say we turn kamikaze. Just fuck 'em all over. Only think about the benefits of our families. What do you say?"

Noodles took another puff from the blunt and closed his eyes. "Before we leave this basement, you and I are going to come up with a master plan to get us to where we need to be. Something ruthless, but strategic and solid. We ain't sparing nothing or nobody. It's all about feeding our starving families, bruh, from here on out. Agreed?" He stood up.

Filipino nodded, then stood up. "Agreed."

They hugged.

Hood Rich

Chapter 6

Mills separated the powder into four thin lines. He took a golden straw and leaned his head down. He tooted one line hard into his right nostril, cleared the path of it, and rubbed the excess off of his nose. He grabbed the bottle of Moët and turned it up. After guzzling a nice portion, he treated his left nostril and scooted back in front of his laptop. Eliza had sent over his father Bronco's current financial records less than an hour ago. He reviewed them closely. He still couldn't believe that the man was worth thirty million dollars. He made investments all over the spectrum. The stock market and real estate fields had been kind to him. His current balance was thirty million and seven hundred thousand. Mills shook his head as he continued to scroll down the log of information. He clicked on the folder of up and coming donations.

Kelly stepped into the room and slid her hands over his shoulders. "What you doing, bro?" She kissed him on the cheek.

"Going over this rich son of a bitch's records. Can you believe he's nearly at thirty one million dollars?"

Kelly sighed. "Christ, that's a lot of money. He was only at fifteen mill like three months ago. How'd he double that?" she wanted to know, paying close attention to the screen.

"I don't know. That's what I'm looking at now. There are a lot of donations in here to nonprofit organizations and churches. Something smells fishy."

Mills continued to look over the records. He was sure that his father was taking part in some sort of money laundering scheme. The records reflected that over the last three months he'd spent fourteen million dollars in donations to so-called charitable organizations. All of them appeared to be within the Crenshaw district where he was employed as an alderman.

Kelly squinted her eyes and read over the records. "Hey, scroll back up once. I want to see what he sent our charity this month."

Mills and Kelly had taken the time to invent a bogus nonprofit organization that specialized in the clothing and housing of the homeless. They did this in an attempt to swindle their father out of large sums of cash. The organization had been invented for six months, and in that amount of time, Bronco Banks had donated two hundred thousand dollars to their cause. Unbeknownst to him, they were the masterminds behind the scam.

"A measly fifteen thousand. That's all he's looking to deposit this month. What a cheap bastard," Mills snapped. He grabbed the bottle of Moët and turned it up.

Kelly shrugged her shoulders. "Looks like it's seventy five hundred apiece, little brother. That's a handbag for me." She rolled her eyes.

"Oh no. I'm not accepting that. You see, Eliza has given me the codes and I have full access to everything. I'll just fudge the numbers a little bit. I'll take a little from here. And a bit from over here. A crumb from here. A few hundred from this one. A piece from this one. And voilà."

Kelly placed her chin into the crux of his neck so she could see the computer. "A hundred grand? You're going to snag a hundred grand? Are you nuts?"

He laughed. "Nope, and it ain't a hundred, it's only an additional eighty five. He won't miss it, and so what if he does? Life is too short to care what Bronco Banks thinks. He can kiss my ass."

There were three knocks in the den's door. "Kelly, are you in there?" Bronco asked.

Mills closed the laptop. He scooted his chair away from the computer and took a handkerchief to cover up the coke on the table. Then jumped out of his seat and answered the door. When he opened it, Bronco's handsome dark-skinned face met him. "Dad, when did you get home?"

Bronco looked his son over and felt a sense of irritation. "Mills, why aren't you at football practice? Have you outright quit the team?" He brushed past him and turned around to face him.

"No, I haven't. I was just on my way there now," he lied. He grabbed his laptop and placed it under his arm. He kissed Kelly on the cheek and rushed out of the room.

Mills hated his old man. They had never gotten along. He felt that he asked way too much of him, that every time his father looked at him, the man felt disappointed. He could feel that deep within his soul. But one day he was sure he would show him. He would show him for all of his utter disdain toward him. Yeah, he was sure that one day he would make him pay.

Bronco stepped into the room and closed the door. He looked Kelly up and down from head to toe. She wore a blue Fendi skirt that fit her like a second skin. The matching halter top accentuated her breasts. He could tell that she was without a bra. Her nipples poked against the material.

"Hey, Daddy. I wasn't expecting you until much later," Kelly said, walking toward him.

Bronco met her in the middle of the room. He grabbed her into his arms, squeezed her ripe backside, and rubbed his hands all over it. "I been thinking about you all day, baby girl. You miss me?"

Kelly moaned deep within her throat. She felt him slowly pulling her skirt above her thighs. "Yes, Daddy. I missed you. You told me that you weren't set to arrive until an hour from now."

Bronco kissed her lips and picked her up. He sat her on the mini bar inside of the den, opened her thighs, and exposed her blue lace panties. He looked into her green eyes as his hand searched under the skirt. His fingers came into contact with warm kitten. "Damn, baby girl."

"What, Daddy?"

"I still can't believe how meaty you are between these legs. That has to be the Italian in you." He yanked her skirt all the way up and kissed her panty's front. He sucked one of her sex lips through the material, then did the other the same way.

Kelly moaned. "What are you doing, Daddy?" She arched her back and opened her thighs wider.

Bronco yanked her panties to the side and swiped his tongue up her pussy's slit. He tasted the juices that were starting to secrete out of her. Then he was eating her kitty with extreme professionalism, opening her folds, paying special attention to her engorged clitoris.

Every time his tongue hit her button, Kelly jerked. She yelped and forced his face further between her legs. "Unh. Daddy. Fuck. Oooh. Daddy. You're..."

Bronco trailed his tongue in circles around Kelly's clit over and over again. He sucked it into his mouth and swallowed the juices that came from her. She tasted salty, and every bit of sweet, unlike her mother, who always left a weird taste in his mouth. Somewhere along the road he'd fallen in lust with his wife's daughter. Now he couldn't help but to think about her every second of every day. Her forbidden body gave him chills.

"Daddy. Uhhh. Uhhh. I'm cumming, Daddy. Baby girl is cumming." She threw her head back and came hard. Her thighs quivered. Her nipples felt as if they were about to pop off of her mounds.

Bronco picked her up and laid her on top of the pool table. He stripped and got between her legs. He rubbed up and down her naked pussy before slipping a finger inside of her box, first one, and then two at a time. Thrusting. He felt her get wetter and wetter. "Daddy gotta have some of this, baby girl. I gotta have some of this. You hear me?" He sucked in her erect clit and flicked it from side to side with his tongue.

Kelly jerked shivered, and opened her thighs as wide as they could go. Her mother's face popped into her mind. It made her feel guilty. Once again she was about to sleep with her husband. It wasn't right. She knew it wasn't. But his tongue felt so good. His penis was so long and thick. He managed to hit regions inside of her body that had only been scratched before. Besides, the wrong in all of it made it so much more sensual for her. It heightened her arousal. "Eat me, Daddy. Unh. Eat your baby. It's okay. It's okay, Daddy."

Bronco fingered her faster and faster. He sucked the juices off of his fingers and slid them back into her. Her cream oozed down to her ass cheeks. He licked it up with his tongue.

"Please fuck me, Daddy. Fuck me now, please. Put that black dick in me."

Bronco loved to hear her beg for it. "Say it again, baby girl. Say it again, but louder this time." His lips wrapped around her clit and sucked ever so lovingly.

She shook. "Come fuck me, Daddy. Come fuck me now. Please!" she screamed.

Bronco stroked his dick and eased the big head inside of her tight slot. The lips opened to accept him. Her heat surrounded him inch by inch until he was balls deep inside of her. He kissed all over her neck and pulled her blouse over her head. Her breasts sprung out. The nipples stood up like erasers. He sucked one, and then the other. He stroked her hard and deep after placing her right ankle on his thigh. Kelly had some of the best pussy he'd ever had in all of his forty-one years of living. He sucked away at her nipple and pounded her out.

"Uh. Uh. Uh. Uh. Uh. Daddy. Aw. Aw. You're fucking me. You're fucking me. Aww. Daddeee." She pulled him down and kissed all over his lips. His dark Jamaican skin contrasted against her tanned Italian skin. His penis burrowed into her garden, slouching in and out of her slippery tunnel. "Harder, Daddy. Harder, Daddy. Harder. Aww. Yes. Yes. Daddeee. Daddeee. Yes!"

Bronco licked all over her lips. He dug deeper and deeper into her body. It seemed to him with every stroke that her pussy got better and better. He couldn't get enough of her.

Kelly dragged her nails across his back. She threw her head back again. "Uhhhhhhhh! Shit, Daddy. Ooooh! I'm cumming."

Bronco slipped his hand between their sexing parts and thumbed her clitoris vigorously. Her pussy began to squirt. That's when he started to long stroke her. His eyes rolled into the back of his head. "Aww, baby. It's so good. It's so good, baby." He pulled out and flipped her on to her knees. He reinserted himself and went back to hitting her pussy hard from the back. *Clap. Clap. Clap. Clap.*

"Aww, Daddy. Fuck me. Fuck me!"

56

Mills opened the door a crack and gazed into the room. He felt his blood boiling. He watched Bronco fuck Kelly for twenty minutes straight, both of them oblivious to his presence. He hated the man. He hated him for cheating on his mother, even though he considered her to be weak. He hated him for corrupting his sister. He hated him for always giving him a look that said the very sight of him disgusted him. He hated the blood that the man placed inside of him. He hated being biracial. He wished that he was full-blooded Italian, that not an ounce of black blood ran through his veins. He yearned for white privilege. He gazed over at them again.

Bronco laid on his back. Kelly bent over and took ahold of his piece. She sucked it into her mouth and proceeded to give him some of the best head of her young life. The sucking sounds drove Bronco crazy, and at the same time infuriated Mills.

"Yeah, baby. Do Daddy. Do me, baby. Fuck, it feels so good. Make me cum in your mouth."

Kelly sucked faster. Her ass was in the air. Juices and cum ran out of her wet pussy. She reached under herself and diddled her clit. Jolts of pleasure courses through her. Then she straddled Bronco and rode him while he sucked her nipples.

Mills shook his head. He slowly eased out of the room and closed the door. "One day I'ma get him back. One day I'ma pay him back for how he's ruining our family," he swore.

Hood Rich

Chapter 7

It was three days after Fancii's model casting and get together. Noodles had still not found the time to take her out
in celebration of her big moment, and it was starting to eat
away at her. She was sitting on the porch, braiding the
neighbor girl's hair from next door, listening to H.E.R.'s
"Shot Clock", when Mills pulled up in a red Range Rover.
He beeped the horn at her and rolled down the passenger's
window.

Fancii felt embarrassed. Her hair was wrapped in a
scarf. She was without makeup, and simply lounging
around in a pair of plain jean shorts and a tank top. She felt
ugly. She had thoughts of jumping up and running into the
house.

Mills beeped the horn again. "Fancii. I see you, baby.
Don't try and hide," he teased.

Nearly every person that was out on Crenshaw seemed
to be looking over at the red Range Rover. A few of the
stick-up kids eyed Mills's whip with hunger. They wondered who was inside, and if he was packing. After those
thoughts passed, they factored in how much time it would
take Mills to be ripped out of the truck and cast aside. There
were chop shops in the area that would buy his stolen truck
for five to ten grand, depending on who you were.

Fancii stood up, and pulled her scarf of off her head.
Her long hair sailed down her back. The light breeze caused
it to flow about in the wind. She stepped over the little girl
and made her way to Mills's attention grabbing truck.
"Mills. What would make you pop up like this? Don't you
remember the boyfriend your sister was telling you that I
have?"

Mills got instantly irritated, but he knew he had to play it off. "Well, I ain't come to see him. I came to continue my pursuance of you. I know you didn't think I would give up on you that easy. You're way too special for that." He popped the locks and pushed open the passenger's door. "Get in, baby. Let's go for a spin."

Fancii didn't know if she liked the sound of him calling her baby. In fact, she knew she didn't. She felt in her heart of hearts that she belonged to Noodles, that she owed him her loyalty, honor, and devotion. They had been through way to much together. "I'm sorry, Mills, but I can't. That wouldn't be proper of me to do such a thing."

Mills hated rejection. He wanted to curse and say something stupid. But then the wind blew and it took Fancii's hair and tossed it all over her pretty face. He'd never seen any female look as radiant as she did in that moment. "Fancii, please. Let's just cruise. As friends. I won't cross any line with you. I won't step on your man's toes. I'll be a perfect gentlemen. What do you say?" His eyes pierced into hers.

She stood there, indecisive. She looked back at the run-down duplex and down to the dirt patch that was supposed to be her lawn, but so many people had tracked across it that it wound up looking like a small field of dirt with grass patches. She saw the little neighbor girl with half of her head braided, and the other half in an afro. Her street was cluttered with gang bangers and dope addicts, people with no dreams, goals, or aspirations. She hated her block, and the dying community as well. She shook her head dejectedly. Life had to be better than this, she thought. Next, Noodles crossed her mind. Then she remembered his promise to take her out after her event - a promise that he'd yet to fulfill. Her anger returned. "You know what, Mills?

Give me a second. I need to go and throw something on a little nicer than this." She turned to jog up the way to her mother's rented duplex.

"Wait. Fancii, you're good. Just come as you are. I'll take care of everything else, I promise."

Fancii touched the scarf off her head. She saw her reflection in the paint of the truck and felt self-conscious. There was no way that she could go out with a distinguished gentlemen such as him self-dressed as she was. It already seemed like every gold-digging female in the neighborhood had their eyes on him. One after the next stepped out on to their porch to see if they could see the man that was driving the red Range Rover. She was afraid that his eye would catch one of them, and because she looked so rough this evening, that he would forget all about her. "Mills, maybe I should go and touch myself up just a little bit?"

Mills smiled. He liked the fact that she was so down to earth. So self-conscious. He opened the door to his truck and stepped out of it dressed in a Gucci short fit with the Gucci sun visor turned backwards. He stepped around the truck and in front of the passenger's door and reached out to take Fancii's hand. "Please, just trust me. I got you."

Fancii saw the females on her block whispering amongst themselves. They laughed at their own mutterings and gave each other high fives. The jackers also whispered amongst themselves, she peeped. She knew they were up to no good. It was in her best interest to get Mills out of there, and fast. "Okay, give me one second." She ran to the porch and picked up the little girl, gave her back to her mother, and promised she'd finish her hair later that night. She grabbed her cell phone off of the porch and then she slid into the passenger's seat and allowed Mills to close the door behind her. The truck smelled fresh, like Cool Water. The leather seats were soft like pillows.

Mills got into the driver's seat and pulled away from the curb. "I can already tell that everything involving you is going to be a fight. I just want you to know that I am prepared for it. Something in my heart tells me that you are worth it." He gazed down at her gorgeous thighs. They were nice and juicy. They looked both soft and firm. He could only imagine what she looked like in the nude. The image caused his penis to stir. He wanted Fancii so bad.

"Oh, you're prepared to fight for me, huh?" That sounded good to her, though she didn't know how true it was.

"I sure am. One thing you're going to learn about me is that I fight for everything that I want until I get it."

"And those are your plans for me too, huh?"

Mills laughed. "I can show you better than I can tell you. A woman like you deserves a fighter. I can look around this neighborhood and tell that you've had to fight for everything you have, and you're fighting even harder to make it out of this hell hole. Is that one of the reasons you are focused on becoming a model?"

Fancii touched the scarf on her head again. She felt so out of place. "Yeah, right now it's my only exit out of this hell hole. I wanna do something to make my mother proud of me. She's struggled to make ends meet ever since my father was deported back to Manilla ten years ago. She deserves better than the hand that she's been dealt. I wanna move her to Beverly Hills one of these days." Fancii sat there for a second and daydreamed about what that would look like. A smile appeared across her face.

Mills got on to the highway and turned up the air conditioner. "That's admirable. Not many people that I know are looking to become a success for another person. They are usually looking for self-gratification. So I seriously I commend your selflessness."

"Thank you. But I don't want you to get it twisted; I am looking to become a success for myself as well. I know that I am more than Crenshaw. I feel that I have greatness inside of me. I want to become successful so that I can come back home and create opportunities for those in my neighborhood. I feel that it is going to take me to change things around here."

"So what about my father?"

"What about him?"

"Well, he's an alderman here in the Crenshaw district, specifically in West Village. He has a lot of political and community support in the entire south side of Los Angeles. Do you think that he will change things for the better when he becomes mayor?"

Fancii shrugged her shoulders. "I think he owes it to the people. They've supported him ever since the beginning. They are going to be the ones that make sure he gets into the mayoral seat. He should make it his business to restore the Crenshaw community – well, the entire south side as a whole. We are dying. Our city is dying. Black businesses are shutting down. Members of our Latino community are being pursued and deported by I.C.E. Gun and gang violence is on the rise. Community centers are being shut down nearly every month. The children are losing places to seek for safe havens. Unemployment amongst minorities is also down by eight percent. I think your father could be a positive asset if he is to get elected. My only fear is that he will forget about the people once he becomes mayor. He hasn't done anything specifically to make me say that. But it's like, very few politicians actually do what they say they are going to do. My prayer is that he is different."

Mills continued to drive, amazed by her intelligence. He wrote her off as just a dumb model that stayed in the ghetto. To hear that she actually had a brain in her skull was refreshing. It also meant that he would have to work a lot harder than he thought.

"I'm sorry, did I offend you? I hope you don't think that I was talking bad about your father. I didn't mean what I said to be taken in a malicious way," Fancii said, pulling down the sun visor so that it protected her from the sun.

"I didn't take it like that at all. I am simply amazed by your intellect. It is attractive to see that you are more than beauty. That's rare - at least speaking on behalf of my en-counters with models." He wanted to take back the line as soon as he said it.

Fancii pursed her lips. "Oh, so you date models on a regular, huh?"

He laughed. Knew he had to keep his cool. The wrong words could cause her guard to go up. If that happened, it would make pursuing her that much more difficult. "I've dated a few. I've never been able to have a connection in-tellectually to any. You are a breath of fresh air. I mean that."

Fancii crossed her arms. She didn't know what to think about Mills. She knew that he as extremely handsome, and wealthy. He drove a nice truck and stayed somewhere amongst the rich. She felt that he could have any woman in the world. She wondered why he'd chosen to pursue her. "Mills, let me ask you a question, and I need for you to be honest with me, okay?"

Mills took the exit and came to a busy intersection. He stopped at the red light and turned to her. "You can ask me anything. I promise to be honest with you as well."

Fancii cleared her throat, looked him into the eyes. "What is making you come after me? I mean, you're handsome. You're wealthy. You frequent the get together spots for models. I'm sure your sister is often your wing woman. She probably helps you get girls all the time, so what is your deal with me?"

The light turned green. Mills stepped on the gas and made a left turn headed toward Rodeo Drive. "I am a physical person first, Fancii. My eyes are my feelers until I get to know a woman. When I first saw you, you literally blew my mind because you are so flawlessly beautiful. The first thing I wanted to do was to get you to be a hostess inside of my gentlemen's club. There is no way that a man would want to leave from my establishment if I had you walking around it in all of your splendor."

"That was your first thought? So why not just ask me if I'd want to play hostess at your spot? Get your answer and go from there?" Fancii asked, confused.

"Because it's like I said, those were my first thoughts. My second thought was that you'd look good on my arm. You looked like you were supposed to be with a man that would spoil you every day of your life. Within minutes of meeting you, I knew I wanted to be that man. That's the truth."

"But Kelly told you that I had a man. That I was spoken for. Why not back away then?"

"Because you are supposed to be in my arm. Any woman worth having is worth fighting for. He's had his chance to show you what he has to offer. Now it's my turn." He pulled on to Rodeo Drive and parked his truck.

He took his father Bronco's credit card out of his wallet. "Fancii, this here is what you would call a black card. We're going to stretch this card to its limit today. Today, we're going to celebrate you. I want to show you a different side of things. Okay?"

Fancii chewed her index finger. She didn't know what to do. She knew what he was proposing, but it didn't seem right for him to being doing what he intended to. Even though Lord knows she was tired of wearing the same out-fit to every casting, she was Noodles's woman. She couldn't give Mills the impression that he had a shot with her. It wasn't fair to Noodles. She sighed and looked out of the window at all of the high end stores that lined the streets on each side. She'd always dreamed of shopping on Rodeo Drive and Sak's Fifth Avenue. She silently wondered if she would ever get the chance again if she turned down this opportunity. She thought she could accept the clothes and make it clear that that was as far as things could go, right? Her head seemed to spin around on her shoulders. She didn't know what to do.

"Fancii, I can tell that you are struggling with a deci-sion. So I'll tell you what. Crenshaw is a long way from here. I'm the driver, and I'm not leaving Rodeo Drive until I spend a nice amount of money on you. You can come along, or you can wait here. Either way, we'll leave in four hours." He smiled. "Or whenever you are completely happy. What do you say?"

She looked at her phone to see if there was any message from Noodles. After confirming that there was not, she be-came agitated. She looked into Mills's handsome face. His eyes peered into hers. They gave her chills. She couldn't deny how fine he was.

"Let's do it. There no harm in shopping right?"

Mills laughed. "None at all."

Hood Rich

Chapter 8

Noodles sat back on the couch with bottle of Patron in his hand. It was three o'clock in the afternoon, and he already found himself both high and drunk. He'd been partying with Filipino and Eddie ever since nine in the morning. Now he was so fucked up that he could barely think straight.

Filipino sat across from him on the couch, equally wasted. His eyes were lower than a basement. He turned up his bottle of liquor and burped loudly. "Damn, cuz, I'm fucked up. We shouldn't have done this shit this early. We gotta make some scratch before the day is over with."

Noodles just wanted to take a nap. He couldn't think about anything else in that moment other than resting. "Man, we will. We just need to get some sleep first. Gotta get some Z's, bruh. I ain't had a good night's sleep in a week. Ain't shit been on my mind but money. That and that bitch nigga, Combo. Why you say he change his name again?"

"'Cause he a sucka, that's why. He got all types of nig-gas trying to buss his head. That fool thinks that if he has multiple aliases that he can evade what he got coming. You know how that shit go." Filipino closed his eyes. Noodles was right. They needed to take a nap. Maybe if they took a nap, it would rejuvenate them.

Eddie came down the stairs and into the basement. He carried a Tech Nine with a fifty round clip. He was short, only 5'5" tall. He was a full-blooded, rather slim, Filipino with a bald head. He had tattoos all over his body and face.. "Guess what, li'l fellas?"

Both Filipino and Noodles kept their eyes closed. The Patron and Maui Loud had them lifted. Noodles was so high that he didn't want to open his eyes. Every time he did, it felt like his high increased. Filipino just wanted to take a short rest. His body was giving up on him.

Eddie cocked the Tech. "That fool Combo just put twenty G's a piece on your heads. He just wants the bodies. He say he'll pay whoever does it forty G's cash. He's extended this offer across the aisle as well. He don't care who does it."

Noodles was the first to open his eyes. The world seemed as if it was spinning. "He just did what?" Noodles stood up and staggered a bit on his feet.

Eddie laughed. "Put up forty G's for your deaths. I could have told you that that was going to happen. Combo ain't nothing but a coward. He ain't a killa. The killas around him are killas. He been like that ever since we went to Crenshaw High. But I'ma tell you what, forty G's is a lot of money to people who ain't got a pot to piss in. Y'all gon have to be on high alert. Straight up." He handed Noodles the Tech.

Noodles squeezed his eye lids together. He licked his lips and prayed the effects of the alcohol and Ganja would ease out of his system. He needed to focus, needed to understand what Eddie was actually saying, because he was so high it all seemed like fantasy to him. But then a part of his brain knew he was in reality. It was crazy.

Filipino opened his eyes and ran his hand over his face. "Cuz, we should go sweat that nigga's crib. That fool always trying to get somebody else to do his dirty work. I'm tired of that shit. Since he got forty G's to spend, that mean he got a whole lot more to lose. What you think, Noodles?"

Noodles walked over to the basement sink. He ran the cold water with one hand and held the Tech with the other. He set the Tech on top of the washing machine and splashed cold water into his face. He did this over and over until his high came down enough for him to focus. After drying his face, he picked up the Tech and walked back into the sitting area of the basement. "Cuz, you know where that fool stay exactly?"

Filipino nodded with his eyes closed. He staggered and plopped down on the couch. "He stay over in Leimert Park with this Mexican bitch. They just had a son. If he gon' be anywhere, that's where he gon' be. I say we ride through Leimert and wet that bitch up like a garden. Show that nigga that it ain't sweet. A dead man can't pay nobody."

"And a dead man can't call no shots either," Noodles chimed in, holding the Tech at arm's length. "You wanna sweat this nigga, I say we do it tonight. Let's catch that fool slipping, and chop that mafucka down like a tree in the forest."

Eddie laughed. "Y'all talking that shit that I like to hear. I ain't never liked Combo. We got history. If anything is going down with him, I gotta be a part of it. But I'll give you one better. What if I told you that I got the low down on all six of his safe houses?"

Noodles felt like he was sobering up. "Cuz, if you got that intel, then fuck getting into a pissing war with this nigga. We need to be hitting his pockets. I'm down for that cash. By any means. What's good?"

Eddie grinned and sat on the couch. "Well, I do know where all six of them are, and whose manning them. Filipino, you know I used to fuck wit' bruh real tough until a few months ago."

"Yeah, until he took Ella from you," Filipino blurted.

Eddie felt himself become instantly irritated. "He ain't take her from me. He got my bitch drunk and smashed. After he did that, I just couldn't look at her the same no more."

"Yeah, who gives a fuck? Anyway, you say that to say what?" Noodles interrupted.

Eddie exhaled and mugged Filipino. He felt embarrassed that Filipino would put his business out into the open like that. "I say that to say I worked closely with him for a number of years. I know how he operates. He's plugged with a bunch of serious connects that got him eating like a fat bitch at a buffet. We can shut down for a few months, focus, and solely look to hit his traps and safe houses. Stack his chips, and take over these streets. I got a few potnas out in San Diego that are looking to make the transition to Los Angeles for whatever reason. I was in Youth Authority with all of them. They are some good dudes. If we are going to sweat this nigga and go at his paper, I wanna holler at my homies and get their assistance as well. What y'all think?"

Noodles shook his head. "Fuck them niggas. We don't need them. Them mafuckas from San Diego. They from the Crenshaw. We two different breeds of killas, bruh. Most of them San Diego niggas are grimy and can't be trusted. We'll fuck around and wind up killing them instead of Combo and his riders, especially if it's a lot of chips involved."

"I'll smoke one of them niggas quick, Noodles. You already know I will. I already don't trust no man outside of you anyway." Filipino reached over and took ahold of the Tech. "I say we do our own thing. If we need further assistance, then we can look outside to San Diego. Right now it's too premature."

Eddie paced the floor. He couldn't believe what he was hearing from the pair. It sounded as if they were already cutting him out of the equation. They must not have understood that he was the one with the intel. He knew how to penetrate Combo. He knew his weaknesses and his strengths. He also wanted to get back at the man worse than the both of them put together. Combo had stolen the love of his life and put a baby inside of her. He wanted to body all three of them because his hatred ran so deep for the man.

"Why the fuck you looking so crazy?" Noodles asked him.

Eddie scoffed. "I don't like what I'm hearing. Y'all making it seem like I won't have a say in how things are going to go. If that's the case, then I might as well use my out of town hittas and handle my bidness. I don't need you niggas." He snatched the Tech out of Filipino's hands.

This pissed Noodles off. "Say, you getting way too emotional, cuz. Ain't nobody cutting you out. We were just saying that we don't know them niggas. That's all. It'll be smarter to get our cash together before we get to outsourcing jobs. Those dudes in San Diego are wild cards. We don't know them, and they don't know us."

"They know me. What part of that don't you get?" Eddie seemed to become more and more hyped up. His face turned crimson. He balled his one fist and scratched his head with the barrel of the Tech. There was a wet spot in the armpit of the right arm.

Filipino yawned. He stretched his arms above his head. "I don't wanna fuck with them niggas, but if it's the only way we make it shake wit' Combo, then whatever. I still say we knock a couple of them first and then pick up the help as needed. The more people we have, the more that the pot has to be split up. I don't know about y'all, but I'm starving right now."

"I thought you fools just hit a major lick for the Maui Loud," Eddie inquired.

"Yeah, but the turnover was only enough to pay a few bills. After paying those for both households, there was barely any left. Mafuckas dealing wit' a few hunnit a piece right now. Bills coming up again. Something gotta shake," Noodles told him, still thinking that Eddie was becoming way too emotional over the San Diego niggas. Something was fishy. He felt that in every fiber of his being.

"Seems like y'all got a problem with money management. That's what that sounds like. We been blowing Loud since early this morning. All of those spoils ain't go to bills. I know we all got a nice amount in our lungs," he scoffed.

Noodles eyed him closely. "And so what, nigga? Life goes on. Now we focus on Combo. You in or you out? It's as simple as that?"

Eddie eyed Noodles. He stepped over to him with the Tech in his hand. "Why you talkin' to me like you all tough and shit, Noodles? Who the fuck do you think I am?"

Noodles tensed up. "Say what?" He stepped into Eddie's face, fearless.

Eddie mugged him. "You heard what the fuck I said. Every time you say something to me, you always say it like you checking me or something. Well, I'm letting you know right now that you ain't checking shit over here, Noodles. Get that through your Jamaican-ass brain right now. Nigga, this ain't that."

"Oh yeah?" Noodles stepped further into his face. His nostrils flared. He could feel his anger bubbling up inside of him. "What is it then, nigga? Huh? What's going on in your Filipino-ass brain?" He balled his fists, ready to bust Eddie in the mouth. He really didn't like Filipino's cousin. In his opinion, Eddie was too emotional. He felt some type of way about everything. He could also sense that he was jealous of his and Filipino's relationship. The fact that he had a Tech Nine in his hand meant nothing to Noodles. Noodles didn't think he had the balls to pull that trigger on him.

Eddie turned his face into a scowl. "Yeah, nigga. You ain't as tough as you think you are. I heard you punched Combo in the mouth, and then ran off like a li'l bitch. That shit don't make you tough. It make you a coward."

Noodles laughed. He anger mounted. His vision became hazy. He took a deep breath and pushed Eddie so hard the he flew over the couch. The Tech slid across the floor. Noodles rushed over and stood above him. "Since I'm a coward, nigga, get yo' punk ass up and show me I'm one. Get up!" he hollered, ready to fuck Eddie over.

Eddie slid backwards on his ass and came to his feet. He balled his fists. He saw how hyped up Noodles was, and a part of him became afraid. Noodles was a man full of muscles. He'd seen him brawl in Crenshaw before and confirmed that he was a savage with his hands. He tried to imagine what things would look like for him in a fight with Noodles, and didn't like what he envisioned. He pulled a Glock Forty from the small of his back and cocked it. "I ain't got hands like you, cuz, but I got heat doe."

Noodles took a step back and mugged him. He wished that he'd come strapped, but he'd left his own weapon under the seat of his Chevy Caprice. He sucked his teeth and looked Eddie up and down. "You got that bitch out, now what you gon' do?" he antagonized.

Filipino jumped in the middle of them. "Whoa, whoa, whoa. Cuz, this shit done went way too far. Ain't no enemies in this room. It's all family in here, am I right?" he asked, looking from one man to the next.

Eddie was ready to pull his trigger. The worst thing a street nigga could do to another killa in Los Angeles was pull a strap on him and not take his life. You never gave another killa a second chance in L.A. Eddie was wishing he'd never pulled the gun. That left him in a tough position. "Cuz, I don't like this nigga always trying to size me up like I'm soft or something. Ain't no pussy in me."

Noodles remained silent. He knew he was going to sweat Eddie over pulling his sword. Nobody had ever pulled a gun on Noodles without him paying them back tenfold. Eddie would be no different. He didn't give a fuck that he was Filipino's cousin.

"Eddie, put that Glock away, cuz. You ain't finna use that bitch on my nigga. That ain't gon happen," Filipino said. If it came down to it, he was willing to knock Eddie's head off of his shoulders over Noodles. In his heart, Noodles was more blood to him than Eddie was.

Eddie held the gun at his side for a moment longer, then slid it into the small of his back. "I ain't got no beef with you, Noodles. We supposed to be family, bruh."

Noodles continued to mug him. In his mind, he was seeing Eddie laying in a coffin with multiple bullet holes all over his body. He wasn't accepting no nigga pulling a gun on him. That could never fly. But there was a way to do everything. He would get Eddie. But it had to be at the right time. Noodles nodded. "I ain't got no beef with you either, bruh. You my dude's cousin. We all family in this room," Noodles assured him.

Filipino smiled. "That's what I'm talking about. Now let's sit down and get an understanding about Combo. He got the riches, and we need the money. A'ight?"

Each man looked around at the others before nodding in unison.

Chapter 9

Fancii was having a bad day. The cash register at the McDonald's where she worked had been acting up all morning. She had a headache and had already gotten into a disagreement with more than one customer over how slow she was carrying on. She felt so angry that she wanted to cry. She pushed the button on the digital screen for a Big Mac again, and finally it popped up. She looked out at the white woman who'd done her share of sighing and smiled at her. "Will that be all?"

The woman rolled her eyes. "Only twenty minutes later. You sure you guys still have the grill on?" she asked sarcastically before handing Fancii a twenty dollar bill.

Fancii took it and rang up the total. The machine beeped three times before she was able to complete the transaction. By the time she finished with it, she was on the verge of tears. She glanced up at the clock and saw that it was five minutes until her break. She stepped away from the cash register just as an Asian man got ready to place his order. "I'm sorry, but I'm on break."

"But you can't just take this last order? I've been waiting for twenty minutes. The customer is always a right."

Fancii wasn't trying to hear none of that. "Sorry, rules are rules. She took her McDonald's cap off of her head and fixed her hair, which was all over the place. She breathed a sigh of relief and came from behind the counter just as Mills was coming through the door with a bouquet of red roses in his hand. The sight of him stopped her in her tracks. "Mills?"

Mills knew that he'd caught her off-guard. He was thankful that Kelly had folded and finally told him where Fancii worked. Upon discovering that it was at a fast food joint, all kinds of bells went off in his head. He felt that trying to get her to work inside of club Flawless was going to be a tad bit easier. All he needed to do was mention better pay and better treatment. He was sure that she would give in. He extended his arm. "These are for you."

Fancii took the roses and felt butterflies in her stomach. She sniffed the flowers and smiled. "How did you know I worked here?"

"Fancii!" the heavyset, dark-skinned male manager called her from the behind the counter. "Your break isn't for another four minutes. Now get back over here and see to these customers. And since you've wasted three minutes, you can deduct those three from your break." He snapped his fingers. "Let's go. Chop, chop, boogie, boogie."

"Sir, I'm sorry." She turned to Mills. "Just give me a few minutes. Let me finish up here."

Mills stepped past her and to the counter. "Is that any way to talk to a Queen? Huh?"

The manager frowned. "What?"

"Mills, please." Fancii pulled on his wrist.

He yanked it away from her. His eyes were laser focused on the manager. "You ungrateful son of a bitch! Don't you ever talk to her like that again. I'll take this minimum wage job and shove it so far up your ass that you'll shit Big Macs for a month!" he snapped.

The manager backed away from the counter. "Fancii, who is this thug?" he asked in fear.

"Sir, I... Mills, please. I need this job," she protested.

"I'm her man, and she quit. She'll never have to work in a hell hole like this ever again. Let's go, Fancii."

Fancii stood there shocked. She didn't know what to do. "But I need to put in my two week notice, and then again, I need this job. My mother depends on me too..."

"You're fired!" the manager yelled.

"Fired?" She was devastated.

"Get out of this store. You've caused enough of a public disturbance for one day. I'm seconds away from calling the police."

"The police?" She gasped.

"Leave this establishment at once." He pointed towards the exits.

Mills took ahold of her hand and pulled her toward the doors. "Let's go, baby. You don't need this job. I got you."

She pulled her hand away from him. "Let me go. And I'm not your baby."

She went into the back room and grabbed her purse and cell phone, then stormed out of McDonald's.

Mills pulled the Mercedes alongside of her and rolled down the window. "Fancii, get in the car, baby." He wanted to get them out of there before the police showed up. The last thing he needed was to engage in some sort of confrontation with law enforcement. He was sure that it would cause major problems for his father's up and coming run for the mayor's seat. While he didn't really care for the man because of how he was carrying on behind closed doors, Mills knew that there was a lot of power in a mayoral seat. Power for Bronco, and power for their family. Power that Mills was thirsty for.

"Leave me alone, Mills. You had no right to get me fired. I needed that job. I'm not filthy fuckin' rich like you. Every paycheck in our family matters." She started to text Filipino's number to ask him to pick her up from work early. She was heated.

Mills threw the car in park and jumped out. He opened the passenger's door of the Benz. "Fancii, get yo' ass in the car. Now. We'll discuss this in a minute."

Fancii was texting away. She stopped and glared at him. Was he serious? Did he think he could talk to her like that?

Mills placed his hand around her waist and guided her into the passenger's seat. "Sit back." He closed the door and jogged around to the other side of the car. He got in and pulled out of the parking lot. "Listen, I didn't mean to get you fired, but you don't need to work at a place where the manager treats you like that. You are a Queen, and should be treated as such."

"Being a Queen ain't gon' pay the bills, Mills. Our rent will be due in two weeks. If I can't come up with my end of the money, I'm basically leaving my mother out in the cold. That's not fair."

Mills reached into his pocket and pulled out a knot of hundred dollar bills totaling eleven thousand dollars. He tossed it on to her lap. It was a portion of the money he'd swindled his father out of for the fake charity that he and Kelly had created. "Here you go. Now can we please move on?"

Fancii picked up the money and thumbed through it. "Wow, how much is here?"

"I don't know," he lied. "It's just some pocket change I had laying around. But it's yours. I just want you to be happy."

She counted five thousand and kept on counting. "I don't mean to sound like a gold-digger or nothing, but hell yeah, this just made me happy. I can pay up the rent and a list of other bills with this."

"You can do what you want it. But I'm putting you up in a condo. Crenshaw is way too dangerous for a Queen like you. I want you to live somewhere where you are safe sound, and I know just the spot." He continued to drive. He had a look of determination on his face.

Fancii sat quietly, counting. When she got to eleven thousand, she gasped in disbelief. "Why are you doing all of this for me? It doesn't make any sense to me. Not even in the least bit."

Mills looked over at her and smiled. "This is what fighting for you looks like. I don't care what I have to do. I'm going to take you away from your boyfriend and make you mines. Once you become mines, I'm going to spoil you every second of every day. Show you the world. Spoil you like you're supposed to be spoiled. I just wanna make you happy." He didn't know for sure if he meant all of those things. In fact, he was sure that he didn't. But to him, Fancii was so beautiful and alluring that he was willing to go the extra mile. Besides, pulling a girl from the ghetto was so easy. All it took was a little bit of money, a few kind words, and they melted. He was conscious enough to know that he represented a journey for her that no man from Crenshaw could offer.

"Well thank you, Mills. Really. I mean it. I'm going try my best to pay you back every penny. I don't know when I'll be able to, but I'm going to definitely try my best."

"Why don't you come and work as a hostess for me? I'll pay you a hundred dollars a night. You can keep all of your tips. And as a bonus, let's say I lease you a '20 Lexus? Truck or car, it doesn't matter to me."

Fancii considered the numbers. A hundred dollars a day wasn't much, but she had no idea how much she could make in tips, or what the job asked of her. The Lexus was an added incentive. She'd wanted to save up for her own car for almost three years, but there was always some bill preventing her from doing that. It was annoying to see how life had her by the throat.

"Well, what do you think?" he asked curiously.

She sighed. "First tell me what would I have to do?"

"You wouldn't do more than greet the customers at the door and guide them to their tables. You'll be the face of club Flawless. That's it; that's all. Maybe in time I'll put you in charge of talent scouting. I would need you to bring in women that are beautiful as you. That's all."

That seemed easy enough to Fancii. "And you're telling me that that's enough to get me paid a hundred dollars a days and to have you lease me a brand new 2020 Lexus?"

Mills nodded. He was already figuring how much cash would be used as a down payment, if any at all. He was thinking that he would have Kelly lease it. If Bronco thought the car was for her, he would probably buy the car outright. If that was the case, Mills would still make it seem as if he was paying the note. He needed to get his hooks into Fancii. There was something about her that he wanted to conquer. "That's all. This ain't about me getting over on you. My ultimate goal is to have you as mine."

Fancii fluttered. Every time he said this she felt guilty and honored at the same time. She really wondered what he saw in her. He could have any woman in the world because of his stature, but he was pursuing her. It made her feel so special. "Well, please give me a day or two to mull this over. I'll get you my answer as soon as I - "

"Talk to him, right?" Mills interrupted. He knew that she'd have to run her possible new job by her boyfriend first. It was cool. He couldn't see the bum being in her life for much longer. All he had to do was continue to turn her on to the good life.

Fancii lowered her head. "Yeah, that."

Mills faked a smile. "It's cool, Fancii. I get it. Just know that whatever you decide, I'ma hold you down anyway. You're special."

She felt her heart skip a beat. She eyed Mills closely. He was lowering her defenses. Every time she spent time with him, she wound up falling for him that much more. "Thank you for saying that. I really appreciate you."

"Hey, I'm just following my heart. It led me to you, and now I'm willing to fight with all of my might to see it through."

***

That night as Fancii sat on the porch of her mother's Crenshaw place, she stared up at the stars and felt saddened. Life had so much more to offer than Crenshaw. There was a whole world outside of what she was used to, a world that she was anxious to penetrate. She really wondered if Mills was the key to her being able to obtain her dreams, or if Noodles would one day get it together so that they could work hard as a team and make it out of the slums like they'd always told each other they would?

Noodles came from the gangway of Fancii's mother's place after leaving the corner store and sat beside her. He kissed her on the cheek. "Hey, baby. What you out here doing?"

She shrugged her shoulders. "I'm just out here watching the stars. Feeling a bit confused about life. That's all. You know how that goes." She took a sip of her vitamin water.

Noodles took a blunt from the inside of his coat pocket and sparked it. The Maui rose into the air in a thick cloud. "Baby, we gon' figure things out. Ain't no sense in you sitting out here stressing yourself about life when tomorrow isn't promised. I got something for you." He pulled two thousand dollars out of his pocket. "Here, this should cover your mother's rent, and some of the utilities for the month. I'm working on something right now that should get us a little further. I just need you to be patient. You ain't gon' be working at McDonald's forever if I got something to do with it." He wrapped his arm around her shoulder. He smelled like Burberry cologne, something that she figured he'd probably stolen. The scent mixed with his body chemistry and made her feel some type of way.

She weaseled out of his embrace and stood up. Her booty shorts had trapped themselves deep within her cheeks. She pulled them out and faced him. "Baby, I want more than this ghetto. I want out of here. Being here every single day is killing me." She felt her eyes begin to water.

Noodles stood up and pulled her into his embrace. "Baby, I know that. I'm working on getting us out of this hood every single day. There is not a morning that I wake up where I don't think about a way to better our situation. You are the driving force within my life. You understand that?"

She nodded. "Yes, baby. Oh, and I don't work at McDonald's no more. I got fired. It's a long story. I don't want to talk about it."

Noodles held her closer. "That's cool. When you're ready to talk, I'm ready to listen. I love Boo. I hope you know that. I don't know what's going on inside of your heart right now, but I need for you to know that I have your back. We are in this impossible life together. You and I, until my last breath. You do know that, right?"

Fancii held him tight. "I know it, baby. I know it. I just wanna get out of here. I wanna get out of this hood so bad and on to something better."

Noodles didn't know what was going on, but he felt deep in the pits of his soul that something wasn't right. "Man, boo, I love you. And I got you. I mean that."

They stood hugging each other in front of Fancii's mother's place as a blue Dodge Caravan slowly cruised down the street. The side door of the van slid open and the shooters got into position. Call it instincts, or call it street smarts. Noodles felt a premonition. He turned and looked down the street just as the van hit the gas and slammed on the brakes in front of them.

"That's yo' ass, Noodles!"

Boom. Boom. Boom. Boom.

Hood Rich

Chapter 10

Noodles threw Fancii to the ground and jumped on top of her, shielding her with his body. "Stay down, baby. Stay down. It's okay. It's okay. I got you."

Boom. Boom. Boom. Boom.

Filipino ran out of the back door of his mother's house and along the gangway with a Mach Eleven in his hands. When he got to the front of the house, he let his tool ride.

Bock. Bock. Bock. Bock.

His bullets slammed into the body of the van and rocked it back and forth. It shattered the windows and knocked out the front headlight closest to the house.

Bock. Bock. Bock. Bock.

The driver of the van stormed away from the curb and sped down the street. All over the block the neighbors were ducked down or laying on the ground all together. Little girls were crying. Boys were saying their prayers. Gun shells littered the pavement.

Fancii struggled to get up. "Get off of me. Get off of me, Noodles. This is the shit I'm talking about." She ran toward the house with tears streaming down her face. She looked to her left, and saw the little nine-year-old girl whose hair she'd just finished braiding that day. She lay on the pavement, her right leg kicking. A puddle of blood formed around her. Fancii rushed over to her and fell to her knees. "Baby, you're okay. Holy shit, you're okay, baby. Oh my God, you're okay," she cried.

Filipino rushed over and helped Noodles up. "Get up cuz. You A'ight?"

Noodles dusted off his knees. "Man, good looking. You was right on time. Them niggas had us dead to wrong." He glanced over and didn't even want to look down.

Fancii picked the little girl up into her arms. She rocked back and forth with her. "All of this killing has to stop. All of this senseless killing has to stop." She wailed.

The little girl's mother rushed out of the house and screamed. "No! No! No! Not my baby. Lord Jesus, not my baby!"

The sirens of the police sounded in the distance. They were only two blocks away. This made both men nervous. The bystanders began to gather around the slain little girl. The life had left her body less than five minutes ago.

"Let's get the fuck out of here, cuz. Twelve on they way. I got this hot-ass Mach in my hand. Let's roll." He jogged back alongside of the house.

Noodles took one look at Fancii. He wanted to go over to comfort her. But time was of the essence. He couldn't afford to be questioned, nor booked by the authorities. In Los Angeles, the police had a habit of whooping your ass before they asked you any questions. He couldn't stand that.

"Noodles. Let's go!"

Noodles took off running behind him with a heavy heart for the little girl.

***

Mills stepped into Club Flawless beside his father's Bronco and looked around. It was eleven o'clock at night and the club was already jumping. There were three regular stages that currently had strippers on them doing their thing to Cardi B's "Money" track. Their asses popped up and down to the beat while their forearms rested on the stage. Mills looked into their cracks and directly at their naked pussies. The patrons tossed dollar bills up at them while the lights in the club flipped from pink, to blue, to yellow, to red, and then repeated the process all over again. There were five waitresses that worked the floor. Their uniforms consisted of two piece G-string bikinis. Bronco made sure that they were flawless and thick as could be with no stomachs. He was a stickler for abs and fit women. When they saw him and Mills they rushed over to them and began to talk amongst themselves. "Can we get you guys anything?" they asked in unison, almost as if they'd been programmed as robots.

Bronco waved them off. "You see, son, all of this is yours. I've taken it as far as I can without overstepping my bounds. You asked me for this club, and now I am turning it over to you. You have to make me proud. Anything you need, I will assist you. Never hesitate to ask me for help. I may not say it enough, but I love you, son." Bronco stepped behind the bar and grabbed a bottle of Ace of Spades. He tore off the gold seal and popped the cork. Fizz bubbled over his knuckles. He poured the liquid into a glass and sipped from it.

Mills couldn't take his eyes off of the Puerto Rican bartender. Her name was Jessica, and to him, she was gorgeous. She was one of the many females that he'd hired that had gone to Beverly Hills high school with him. He winked at her.

She blushed and tended to a customer. When she turned around, he saw that her tight skirt was hugging her ass. The cheeks jiggled out of the bottom. Her thick thighs were mesmerizing. He needed to get laid. It had been a few weeks. All of the chasing of Fancii had taken him off the course of meaningless pussy chasing.

"Son, my only question to you is, do you think that you are ready to step into the role of a leadership position here at Club Flawless?"

Mills had to shake the cobwebs out of his brain. It was important that he tuned into everything that his father was saying. After all, Bronco was the one funding the club. He cleared his throat. "Yes, Dad, I am. I have a vision that will take Club Flawless to the next level. This is one of the only jobs I can see myself doing where I will still be able to maintain my education while I am acting as CEO. As you know, it is my dream to become an affluent businessman and real estate mogul such as yourself."

This made Bronco smile. Nothing sounded better to him than hearing his son saying that he wanted to follow in his footsteps. That, he felt, was every successful man's wish. "Those words alone aren't enough to make me proud, son. You must show and prove with actions."

Mills felt irritated. *Here goes the lecture*, he thought. Before the old man could get started, he cut him off. "Dad, all I need is for you to give me a shot. Have faith in me. I won't allow this opportunity to slip through my fingers. You'll see."

Bronco laid his hand on Mills's shoulder. "I know you won't, son. I trust you. But for the first year, or until you can show me by actions, I am going to occasionally peek over your shoulders. I'll drop by the club unannounced. I'll be a thorn in your side. Anything that goes wrong in this club falls back on my shoulders, and my campaign. So you are holding a lot of weight for this family. Do you understand that?"

Mills didn't like Bronco resting his hand on his shoulder. The only vision he could muster inside of his brain was that of Bronco fucking Kelly on the pool table. It was enough to make him vomit. But he knew he had to stroke the old man's ego until he got what he wanted out of him.

It was the only way. "Dad, the campaign is not more important to me than you are. I strive to make you proud. You have been my hero ever since I was a very little boy. All I ask is for you to show a little faith in me."

Bronco squeezed his shoulder and smiled. "Okay, son. I'll do just that. You've got my word on that." He laughed and hugged Mills.

Mils frowned throughout the entire hug. He hated the man touching him. Bronco repulsed him in every single way. He reminded him of a worse version of R. Kelly without the music. Mills had watched him screw Kelly on at least fifty separate occasions throughout the years, dating all the way back to when she was just a young teen. He patted his father's back. "I love you, Pops. I swear I do."

***

It was two o'clock in the morning when Fancii finally stepped from the shower, trying her best to wash the night's event off of her. She'd been questioned by more than one police officer, and more than one strategy had been used upon her. She was tired of talking. Tired of crying. Tired of the ghetto of Crenshaw. She was depleted. After drying herself off and getting dressed, she eyed her bed as a cloud of heaven. She couldn't wait to stretch out and call it a night. She sat on the edge of the bed and set her alarm clock for eight the next morning. She had to be at the area's technical college first thing in the morning. She pulled back the covers and clicked off the lamp, and nearly jumped out of her skin when Noodles tapped on the window.

Noodles looked both ways outside. He had two Forty Glocks on his hip and a bulletproof vest across his chest. Now he was prepared for another try on his life whereas before he had not been. Ever since he'd left Fancii's side, he couldn't get her out of his system.

Fancii pulled up the blinds and saw him. She felt like closing them. How could he have run out on her earlier? How could he leave her alone in such a vulnerable state of mind? She wanted to snap, and emotionally she was unavailable for him. She raised the window. "What do you want, Noodles?"

Noodles felt offended. "Damn, what's wrong with you?"

She smacked her lips. "Look, I gotta get up for school early in the morning. I ain't got no time for this right now. Holler at me later." She closed the window and lowered the blinds. Her phone buzzed. There was a text from Mills that said, "I'm up thinking about you. I hope you're okay, Queen." That made her smile. She felt like picking up the phone and Facetiming with him.

There was a knock on her bedroom door, then it opened before she could answer it. Noodles walked into her bedroom and closed the door.

"I see you can't take a hint." She rolled her eyes.

"What the fuck is wrong with you, Fancii? You been acting real funny toward me for a few days now. What did I do to you?"

"Noodles, I don't feel like getting into this right now. A lot has happened today. I need to clear my mind. I'll talk with you tomorrow." She got up to pull the door open, determined to get him out of her bedroom so she could Facetime with Mills for a few minutes. She just needed to communicate with somebody outside of the ghetto, and Kelly wouldn't be enough. She would only make her yearn for Mills, as much as she hated to admit that.

Noodles snatched her up and carried her back into the room. She fell on the bed with him between her thighs. He grabbed both of her wrists and held them to the bed.

"Fancii, you are my woman. I am your man. We belong to each other. I wanna know what's going on with you. Damn, this shit is tearing me apart."

Fancii was crying. She could no longer stop the tears. "I want out of this hood, Noodles. I want a better life. I'm tired of the senseless killings. Tired of being poor, and struggling for everything that I have, and never having enough. There is pain inside of me that runs deep. I'm so tired." She began to sob.

Noodles was shocked. He fell off of her and pulled her into his arms. "Baby, I know. I know, baby. It's hard right now, but I'm going to get us out of this hood. It's on me to make it happen, so that's what I'm about to do."

"How, Noodles? How are you going to do it? You can't get away with what you've been doing forever. Sooner or later your luck is going to run out, and so is Filipino's. Then what will I have? What will I do?" she cried. "I can't take care of my mother on my own and myself too. That's too much pressure. I feel like I'm drowning as it is." She cried harder.

Noodles hated to hear any female in his life that he cared about cry. It made his soul bleed. He rolled her on to her back and kissed her neck, sucking on it.

"Stop, Noodles. I don't feel like it right now. I'm hurting."

"I know, baby. I got this." He licked along its length and sucked harder. He took ahold of her tank top and pulled it over her head. "We in this thing together, baby. Me and you. I'ma make it happen for us. I got to. It's always been me and you since the beginning. Ain't I right?" More kissing.

"Yes, baby."

His hand snuck between her golden thighs. He spread them and rubbed the front of her panties. The cloth slipped inside of the material. Her sex lips appeared on each side of the crotch band. He scooted down and sniffed her cat. He licked the crotch and pulled the material to the side, exposing her garden. Her kitty was engorged, the lips plump and a shade of golden red. Her scent rose to his nose and caused him to shake. He played his finger over the slit and sucked it into his mouth.

Fancii arched her back and raised her crotch, offering herself to him inadvertently. "Noodles. Please. Noodles."

His tongue slid past her sex lips again and again. Then he was sucking her pearl, driving her crazy. Her juices dripped off of his chin as he pleased her. He wanted to make her feel better, needed her tears to cease until he could figure out how he was going to change their situations. He loved her far too much to know she was hurting and do nothing about. His sex game had always healed her, and he was hoping for more of the same.

"Noodles. Noodles. Aww. Please," Fancii moaned. She squeezed her breasts together and jerked forward. She looked down, and saw his head between her legs going from side to side. The sight was enough to push her over the top. She fell backward as the ripples of an intense orgasm rocked through her with no mercy. "Uhhhhhhhh! Noodles."

Noodles sucked on her clit while she went berserk. She forced his face further into her crotch, wrapped her thighs around his face, and humped into his mouth over and over, cumming hard. Then she fell on her back. Noodles lay beside her, playing with her wet pussy. The lips opened like the petals of a flower on a rainy day.

"I love you, Fancii. I'ma fight for you, baby. I'ma fight to get us out of this ghetto. You are my everything. I want you to know that." Two fingers skipped inside of her leaking kitten.

She arched her back again, yearning for him to climb atop her and finish what he'd started. But then the image of the little girl laying on the pavement twisted was enough to knock her out of her sexual zone, and it became an emotional one. "Noodles, baby? Can you hold me for the night?"

Noodles's penis was throbbing in his pants. He wanted some of her treasures bad. He needed them. Was aching for them. "Sure, baby. That's all I wanna do anyway," he lied. "I just wanna hold you all night through because I love you." He pulled his fingers from her box and sucked them into his mouth, savoring her juices.

Fancii allowed him to spoon behind her. She scooted backward into his lap and laid her head on a pillow. Noodles kissed all over the back of her neck, telling her how much he loved her, and how he would fight for her. A short time later she was out cold, and he followed suit thirty minutes afterwards.

Hood Rich

Chapter 11

Filipino grabbed Noodles's wrist and nearly dragged him into the basement. When they got to the bottom step, Filipino pointed at the couch.

"Noodles, we don't need Eddie when we got her."

Sky sat on the couch with her thick, caramel thighs crossed. Her hair was cut into a short, curly style. The sides were shaved. She stood up, all 5'5" inches of her. She placed her hands on her hips and popped back on her legs. She was fine and she knew it. She eyed Noodles from across the room and smiled.

Noodles slowly stepped into the portion of the basement where Sky was sitting. Sky was Cheyenne's best friend. She and Noodles had dated for a short period when they were in the sixth grade. It was mostly innocent, though they had done some harmless touching. He hadn't seen her in the physical in nearly eight years. She looked amazing. "Sky?"

She smiled and batted her eyelashes. "If it isn't Nadell." Nadell was Noodles's first name. "Or should I say, Mr. Noodles himself?" She walked over to him and gave him a hug.

The scent of her perfume reached him before she did. She smelled good to Noodles. Tantalizing. He hugged her and kissed her on the cheek. "Long time no see. How have you been?"

She slid from his arms. "Oh, I'm doing fine. I'm into the Weed Dispensaries. Got myself an old white man who spoils me. Doing the real estate thing a li'l bit as well, but to be honest, I miss the hood. I ran into Filipino a few hours ago, and we hit it off. Word is that you're trying to fuck over Combo. I want in. You know what he did to my brother."

Two summers ago back in 2017, Sky's younger brother Mac had tried to rob Combo and a member of his crew. There was a scuffle, and Mac wound up getting shot three times in the face. Combo was acquitted of the murder because one of the many cameras in Baldwin Village had caught footage of the entire ordeal. Noodles was told that Sky had taken it hard. He'd been visiting relatives in San Francisco when all of that took place.

"Hell yeah. Man, we heard that Combo got a whole list of traps that's making some serious cash. He got shit spread out all over Los Angeles and we need to find a way to bust that shit up, and it'll be easier if we can penetrate his circle. You think you can help us with that?"

She sat on the couch and crossed her thick thighs. Her short Burberry skirt pulled back on her thighs. They were freshly oiled up and glistening. She took a fat, stuffed, Cuban cigar out of her purse and set the tip ablaze. Thick clouds of smoke billowed toward the ceiling. "You bet yo' bottom dollar that I can help you. I'ma call in a few favors. Get my girls to link up with a few of his security team. We gon' find out the ins and outs of everything. Just give me a few days. In the meantime, I have a lick for you boys that could gross you ten grand apiece. Are you up to it?" she asked, passing the blunt to Noodles.

Noodles took it and sniffed the smoke. He needed to make sure that it was marijuana that she was smoking, and nothing was mixed with it. "Say, shawty, this just bud, right?"

Sky frowned. "That's OG Kush, pure and sprayed. It's the best in all of California. I'm smoking that shit that the rich politicians are smoking. Try it out," she encouraged.

98

Noodles sniffed the smoke again and took three deep pulls. He held the smoke, and it became so harsh that he wound up blowing it out and choking at the same time. His lungs felt raw, as if he'd inhaled a pot of boiling water. His face turned a bright shade of red.

"Aw, hell n'all." Filipino grabbed the blunt from him and took four deep pulls slumping on to the couch. His chest felt just as raw. His eyes burned. He held the smoke for as long as he could. Then he was coughing and falling to his knees. Tears rolled down his cheeks. Smoke came out of his nose and mouth at the same time. It looked like his face was on fire.

Sky busted up laughing. She snatched the blunt away from him and took two light pulls off of it. She was already higher than the roof of a house. "That's the kush, baby. You gotta respect it, or it'll leave your asses twisted like you two niggas." She got to laughing louder and louder. The weed only enhanced her funny bone. "Awright, now that y'all done got buckled by my shit, it's time we talk jobs. There is twenty gees on the table if you want it. Ten apiece. Should we sit here and get an understanding?"

Noodles took a sip of his apple juice. His eyes were redder than cherry Kool Aid. He could barely breathe without feeling like his lungs were being ripped out of him. "I need that li'l ten. I'm in, I don't give a fuck what I gotta do."

Filipino eyed her thick thighs and struggled to breathe normally. "Me too. I ain't never turning down no new money. What we doing, smoking somebody?"

"Not for no twenty gees," Noodles interrupted him.

"Of course not," Sky assured them. "I just want you to break a few bones. And make my message clear. You see, there have been a few thugs that have been trying to squeeze and strong arm two of our dispensaries. Saying that me and my old man must pay them ten grand a week per dispensary. That shit ain't happening." She pulled up their addresses on her cell phone and handed the phone to Noodles.

Noodles looked it over. "These niggas stay in Compton. We'll breeze through there with no problem. What you trying to do?"

"Like I said, just shake 'em up a li'l bit. Let them know that fucking with Addison's Dispensaries will put them in a fucked up position. You feel me?"

Filipino sat on the couch next to her and placed his hand on her knee. "I wish I could feel you. You done got thick as hell, Sky. What the fuck you been eating?" His hand traveled to her inner thigh.

Sky parted them. Filipino was all the way under her short skirt now. His fingers ran up and down her pussy lips, which were covered by the material. "I been eating a lot of soul fool. I moved my mother up here from Atlanta, and she dead set on putting some meat on my bones."

Filipino's fingers slipped through the leg hole of her panties. He pulled her thigh on his lap, moved the panties to the side, and started to finger her pussy fast. It got wetter and wetter, until his fingers were slouching in and out of her.

"Oooh. Oooh. Shit. Fuck. Come here, Noodles. Please." She opened her thighs wider.

Noodles caught sight of her pussy. It was nice and trimmed. The sight of it caused him to become harder than a block of wood. He walked over to her and stopped directly in front of her. "What's good, shawty?"

Filipino sped up the pace. He started to finger her so fast that his wrist became a blur. She was leaking as if she was peeing on him. "You miss this hood shit, don't you? Tell me you miss this hood shit?" he growled.

She threw her head back and moaned loudly. She reached out and grabbed Noodles's dick through his pants, squeezed his log. To her it felt like a ripe cucumber. "Noodles. Let me suck it. Aww fuck. Let me suck it, Noodles."

Noodles backed up and smacked her hand away. "I'm fucking wit' Fancii now, Sky. I can't cheat on my baby like that. Y'all do ya thing."

Filipino stood up and yanked her skirt up her hips. He ripped her panties from her frame and tossed them to the side. He took his hard dick and slid into her balls deep."

"Uhhhhhhhh! Shit, Filipino!" Sky screamed. Her nipples were fully erect, poking at her Burberry blouse. She was without a bra.

Filipino pulled her blouse over her titties and sucked on the nipples while he fucked her with long, hard strokes. She was tight and wet. Her walls clung to him. They sucked like a lubricated vacuum cleaner. He slouched in and out, sending juices into her asshole.

"Uh, Filipino. I miss this hood shit. I missed it. Uh, damn. Fuck me, nigga, shit." She raised her ankles until they were on his shoulders.

Filipino really got to hitting her hard then. His dick shot in and out of her box at full speed. Beating down her walls as if he was renovating. "Huh. Huh. Huh. Huh. Gimme this pussy, bitch. Gimme this shit. Uh. Fuck," he growled, hammering away.

Sky took the pounding. She opened her eyes and looked over to Noodles. His dick was rock hard, sticking up against his pants. She wondered what it looked like, wondered how fat it was, wondered what he would taste like. She'd had a major crush on him ever since they were kids.

His dark skin drove her crazy. He was so fine. She watched him adjust his dick inside of his pants as Filipino pounded away at her.

Filipino sucked her left nipple hard. He pulled it with his lips until it was distended. Then his tongue twirled around it. He plunged and plunged.

Sky cried out. "Aw shit. Aw shit. I'm cumming! I'm cumming! Uhhhhhhhh! Fuck!"

Filipino was a battering ram. He smashed that pussy, fucked her as hard as he could. There was a constant smacking sound that emitted from between her crashing middles. He tensed up as his seed built up deep in his belly, and then he was releasing it into her.

She felt his seed hitting her walls. The feeling sent her into another wave of orgasms. Her nails dug into his back. She licked at the sweat of his neck. Her eyes opened again and went into those of Noodles. The sight of his handsome face gave her tingles as her orgasms slowly faded into a series of jerks.

Filipino pulled out of her box and stood up with his greasy dick jumping in the air. "We gon' handle this bidness for you first thing in the morning, and you make sure that you have that twenty bands ready to go. After we get done hollering at them, you ain't gon' have to worry about them clowns no more. Ain't that right, Noodles?"

Noodles needed to go to the bathroom to relieve himself. He watched Sky sit on the couch rubbing her pussy, and it was driving him crazy. She locked eyes with him and spread her brown pussy lips. Her insides were bubblegum pink. "You damn right. Look, I gotta piss, bruh," he lied. "I'ma fuck wit y'all in a minute." He jogged up the stairs and into the bathroom. Closed his eyes and got right while he imagined the sight of Sky's fat pussy.

Filipino stepped over and fed her his piece. "Come on, shawty, go 'head and suck them juices off of there for me. Let me watch them pretty lips work.

Sky grabbed his tool in her fist, pumping it. "Y'all gon' get me right? Huh?"

Filipino grabbed a handful of her hair. "You already know it. Just handle this bidness first, and then we gon' handle yours."

Sky licked around his head. "Okay, baby, I gotchu." She sucked him into her mouth and drove him crazy for ten straight minutes until he came down her throat. She popped him out. "One of them niggas stole my locket. Get my locket back and it's an extra five in there for you. My father gave me that locket before he passed away. It's the only memory I have of him that was sentimental to me."

Noodles came down the steps, freshly relieved. "Well, we gon' get that back for you. You holler at your girls about Combo, and we'll jump on this for you like a-sap."

Sky smiled and looked into Noodles's eyes. "That's what I wanna hear."

Chapter 12

"Say, li'l homie, y'all got that OG kush up in there? Me and my mans heard that y'all got that heat fresh from the dispensary. What's really good?" Noodles asked.

The Pusher looked him up and down. "Nigga, how you know so much about me and my operation?" he asked.

"So that's a yes or a no on the OG kush, li'l homie?" Filipino inquired as the sunlight shone off of his forehead.

The Pusher mugged him. The scent of bacon and eggs emanated from his out of his one level crib. There were two other young dudes about his age playing Fortnite on the big screen television. His baby mother cooked breakfast food in the kitchen. "Nigga, you acting like you got an attitude problem. How much money you niggas got, bruh?"

Noodles grabbed his pistol from the small of his back and slammed it into the Pusher's forehead. Bam. The handle broke through the skin and busted his head wide open. Blood ran down his cheeks. He flew backward into the house, his arms wagging in the air.

Filipino rushed in with both Forty Glocks out, locked and loaded. "All you bitch-ass niggas lay the fuck down. Y'all already know what this is, cuz."

The two young men that were playing Fortnite fell to the floor. They stretched their hands above their heads. Both were shaking, preparing for the worst and hoping for the best. The Pusher's baby mother ran into the back room. She grabbed her baby out of the crib and sank to the bedroom floor with him after closing the door. She was terrified. Something had told her to not spend the night with her baby father. He was always getting into something.

Noodles was on her heels. He broke through the door with a loud crash and aimed a gun at her. She screamed. This caused her son to begin crying.

"Listen, shawty, I ain't gon' hurt you. This shit ain't about you. But I'ma need you to come in here and lay on yo' stomach so we can take care of what we need to. Come on, shawty." He pulled her up and led her back into the living room.

Filipino had everybody's ankles tied and their hands behind their backs by the time he made it back into the living room. He even had their mouths taped - all except the Pusher. He turned to him and smiled. "Bruh, I got all these bitch niggas laid out, it's good."

Noodles laid the female on her stomach and tied her ankles and wrists. The baby was crying and screaming like crazy. He didn't know what else to do so he sat her son in her arms. "Shawty, you good. Its awright. Matter fact..." He took the tape off of her wrists. "Just quiet him down so this process can go a lot faster."

She nodded at him. "Okay." She held her son in her arms and rocked him back and forth. "Shhh. Shhh. Quiet now, baby. Quiet. Mama is right here. You're safe, baby." Slowly but surely, the baby became calm. She raised her shirt and fed him her left nipple and then he was quiet, sucking away.

Noodles grabbed the Pusher up by his dreads and slammed him against the wall. He placed his Glock against his nose. "I heard through the grapevine that you mutha-fuckas got a problem with Addison Dispensaries. Is that true?"

Blood ran out of the Pusher's forehead and along his neck. "I don't know what the fuck you talking about, cuz. I ain't fucked with no dispensary."

Noodles smacked him as hard as he could with the Glock, so hard that the skin tore and bled. He forced his forearm under his throat. "You wanna try that fuck shit again? Huh?" He choked him with his forearm, and then released him.

The Pusher's knees buckled. His head was already swelling up like a strawberry. "Okay, okay, my nigga. I know what you talking about." Blood ran from his nose. "I know what you talking about."

Noodles picked him back up. "What's your beef with them?"

He struggled to breathe through his nose. He could be heard wheezing. "I ain't got no problem with them as long they pay their fees. This Los Angeles, homie. Everybody gotta pay somebody in order to stay in bidness. Ain't no such thing as free enterprise. You know how the game go. Ever since they legalized weed in this state, it's dispensaries popping up all over the place. I'm just getting in where I fit in. Plus that bitch owes me."

Noodles punched him in the stomach and flung him to the floor. He stepped on his neck, pressing down on it with his blue Chuck Taylors. "What the fuck she owe you for?" He added pressure to his foot, and then took it away.

His baby mother had tears running out of her eyes. "Please don't kill him. Please don't kill him, mister." She closed her hands in a prayer fashion.

Noodles zoomed in on the gold locket around her neck. The heart of the locket was encrusted with yellow diamonds. It sparkled and glistened in the light of the house.

Noodles gripped her forehead, and grabbed the locket from around her neck, yanking it away with one tug. He mugged her. "Do you know that he could have gotten you killed for this shit you're wearing around your neck? Huh?"

She shook her head as her baby sucked away at her nipple hungrily. It popped the one out of its mouth and latched onto the other one, leaving the first one erect and covered in spit. "He gave that to me for my birthday," she cried. "It's the nicest thing anyone has ever done for me."

Filipino stood over her. "Yeah, well, that nigga stole that from an innocent woman. A woman whose father gave it to her. She gotta have her shit back. That's how that shit gon' go. Yo' man a dirty-ass nigga. Straight up."

The Pusher fell to his back and curled into a fetal position. There was so much blood around him that it looked as if he'd been doused in burgundy paint. "That bitch ain't innocent. She knows what she did to my brother." He winced in pain, grew dizzy, and fainted.

Noodles bucked his eyes. He looked over to Filipino in a panic. He didn't know what to do. They weren't expecting to come in and stank anybody. All they wanted was to strike fear into the Pusher and his crew so that they didn't screw around with Sky and her man's dispensaries anymore. But if The Pusher bled out, they were looking at murder. That meant that the entire household would have to go.

"Man, fuck that nigga. Look, y'all stay the fuck away from Addison Dispensaries. It's as simple as that. If we find out that you li'l niggas been fucking around with them again, it's gon' be a problem. Y'all dig me?"

The two on the floor nodded in unison. The Pusher's baby mother nodded her head as well. She just wanted to get him up and to the hospital. She would talk to him about leaving the psychos that were Noodles and Filipino alone. "Please, can I get him to a hospital?" she cried. This caused the baby to break into a fit of screams again.

Noodles kicked the Pusher in his ass. He didn't move. He kicked him again. "Say, nigga, get yo' ass up. Get up, homie, stop playing." Still there was no movement from him.

Filipino stood over him. He knelt down and put his finger to his neck, felt a weak pulse. "Man, this nigga's still alive. I don't know for how much longer though. You wanna risk this shit, cuz?" He stood up, looking at Noodles.

Noodles scratched his waves. "Fuck. Fuck. Fuck. If this nigga dies, we looking at murder one. Then they got three witnesses to put our ass in the gas chamber. Fuck."

"Four if you count that baby," Filipino added.

"No. I swear to God, me and my baby ain't got say nothing. Please don't take our lives. We ain't got nothing to do with none of this. I am begging you."

Filipino stepped over her. "Bruh, try that nigga's pulse again. If it ain't there, we gotta do what we gotta do. It's as simple as that."

Noodles knelt and placed two fingers against the Pusher's neck. Now there was no pulse. He checked all around for one, and came up empty. He stood up and scratched his head with the barrel of his gun. "Uh, bruh, that fool dead. We got a major problem."

Filipino grabbed the silencer out of his left front pocket and screwed it into his weapon. "Nall, it's plain and simple what has to go on here. Fuck that nigga. I ain't finna let his situation throw my life away." He aimed the gun at the two dudes that were tied up on the floor. "It's over, bruh.

They began to scream into their duct tape. The rolled around on the floor like trapped worms. The Pusher's baby mother wailed.

Filipino was having none of it. He gave the dudes facials. Two apiece, right through the forehead. Then he stood over the mother. "Bitch, move that shorty or both of y'all gon' get it." He was in a murderous rage.

Noodles couldn't watch this part. He felt some type of way towards the mother. He didn't want to see her or her son be harmed, but he knew what was at stake. "Hey, bruh, I'll meet you in the car."

Filipino waved him off. "Yep." He looked back down at the Pusher's baby mother. "Look, shawty, you gotta go. Blame this shit on yo' nigga. He brought this dishonor on your household.

"Please. Just. Can you just let us live. I won't say nothing. I swear in my..."

Filipino aimed at her and squeezed three shots. She dropped the boy. He fell to the ground, crying his heart out. Filipino turned and ran out of the back door, trailing Noodles.

***

Later that night, Noodles sat in front of Cheyenne and Sondra. They were seated in the living room with the big screen playing. Noodles counted the fifteen thousand dollars in front of them that Sky had given him. Ten for the lock, and five for recovering her locket. A'ight, ma, we should be able to go ahead an additional six months on the rent and utilities. That'll take us out of the year. There is three thousand and five hundred dollars left over. I'm giving you a G, Cheyenne, so you can pay your car note, and the insurance. The rest can be your pocket change, I guess. Mama, I'm giving you fifteen hundred because you'll need five for groceries, and the G is for your pocket. You know you're my baby."

"Thank you, sweetie," Sondra said, smiling across the glass table at him.

"Yeah, thanks, li'l bro. You always come through for me," Cheyenne added. She came around the table and hugged him and kissed him on the cheek. "When I get paid I'll give you a few bucks of that paycheck so I can start paying you back." She kissed his cheek again and made her way to the back of the house toward her room.

Sondra stepped to the old school record player and placed an Isley Brother's record on the table. Their "For the Love of You" track bellowed out of the speakers. She two-stepped and then came around the table and took his hand. "Aw yeah, baby, it's time you dance wit' Mama. It's been a long time." She took ahold of her son and hugged closely to his body.

Noodles held her by the hips and allowed her to lay her head on his chest. As a young boy, and even a teen, he'd always danced with her whenever she called to him. He liked to see his mother in a good mood. She particularly loved to dance once she knew that all of the bills were taken care of.

She kissed his cheek. "You've always been a good son, Noodles. You've always taken care of your mother, and I love you for it." She rested her head on his shoulder. They continued to groove together.

"Mama, I love you so much. I'ma take you out of this hell hole. I'm working on something right now to make it to so we never have to worry about the ghetto again."

These words frightened Sondra. She knew what Noodles was capable of, but she didn't like him doing crazily things just so he could solidify their futures. She wished that she could help him, wished that she could get a job so she could take some of the pressures off of him. She knew that Noodles was crazy about her, that he was overprotective. He was a provider at heart, and wanted to see the best for his mother, and sister, even more so than for himself. While that made her feel special and loved, it also terrified her to the very core of her soul.

"Mama, how much you say one of those nice houses in the suburb gon' cost us?" Noodles dipped her and pulled her up, holding her to his chest. His mother was his angel.

"Nearly a million dollars, Noodles. Where the hell are you going to get that kind of money?" she asked.

"I don't know for sure, but for you, I know I'ma get it. I'm getting you up out of this hood. You deserve your own throne, your own palace, Mama. I got you. Please just know this. We been struggling for way too long."

Sondra buried her face into his shoulder. "I know, baby. I know. But things will get better when God says it's time. We can never rush the good Lord. Nothing good ever happens when you rush the Lord."

Noodles believed in God, but he also felt that nothing was just given to you. Not even from the Lord. He felt that a man's job was to go out and get it by any means. He didn't think that even God respected men that sat around on their asses and let God to do all of the work for them. No, in his mind he knew that God only blessed those men who went out and got it for themselves. He was doing that the best way he knew how, and he felt no remorse because he had to. He took a deep breath and continue to vibe to the music with her. He placed his lips close to her ear. "When a boy becomes a man, Mama, he is supposed to go out into the jungle and survive by any means. The mother that raised him is supposed to work no more. She is supposed to get everything that she desires in life through him. It's been you, me, and Cheyenne for the longest. You've been busting your butt for us ever since that man walked out on you. Mama, I owe you my life. It's as simple as that."

Sondra inhaled and slowly blew that breath out. She didn't know what to say. Her son had become a man. He wanted to provide for the family and get her a palace. She appreciated that. What mother wouldn't? She stepped closer to him and kissed his cheek again. "Baby, just be careful out there. Be careful, and be smart. I need you. You are my only son." She took a step back and looked into his eyes as the music continued to play out of the speakers. "Do you hear me, Nadell?"

He stared at her for what seemed like a long time without answering. Then slowly his face turned into a smile. "Yes ma'am. Come here." He pulled her to him, and they continued to dance to the Isley Brothers.

Chapter 13

It was a hot and sunny afternoon. Mills pulled his Mercedes Benz into the long driveway of his parents' estate. He threw the car in park, but before he could take the key from the ignition, Kelly jogged out of the mansion and knocked on the passenger's window of his car. He frowned and rolled down the window. He had a slight migraine after jogging alongside the beach with nothing to drink. He felt dehydrated and tired. All he wanted to do was get into the shower and drink a gallon of filtered water.

Kelly tried to open the car and found it locked. She knocked on the roof. "Mills, open the fucking door. I gotta talk to you before you got into the house. Dad is losing his fucking mind."

Mills sat up and popped the lock. "Losing his mind for what?" he asked, getting irritated already.

Kelly slid into the car and plopped down. The heavy scent of her Chanel perfume filled the interior. She dragged her fingers through her hair and flipped a nice portion of it over her shoulders. "Mills, he knows about the fake charities."

"What? How could he possibly? Dad's a fucking idiot when it comes to all of that shit. He has way too much going on." Mills began to panic.

"He didn't figure of out. It's that bitch Eliza that you told him to hire. She found all of the fake charities that we've created over the years, and now they're going over the financial records and tracing all of the withdrawals. I'm so scared that I feel like leaving home and never coming back. Fuck. And Dad used his leverage to get me a role on the CW, and three pages in *Elle* magazine. Shit, this sucks."

Mills rubbed his chin. There had to be a way out of this. He couldn't allow them to throw in the towel. He just couldn't. There was always another move. He was glad that he'd just withdrawn the last forty thousand dollars from the account before it was flagged by Bronco and Eliza. What the fuck was Eliza's crazy ass thinking anyway? He wished he would have explained things to her more clearly instead of beating around the bush. It seemed that it would have saved them a world of trouble. He knew it was about to go down.

"I'm just going to come clean and beg for mercy. With any luck he'll do some yelling, and then this will pass. Its only money, right?" Kelly looked to Mills.

He pursed his lips and looked at her like she was stupid. "Not for Bronco Banks. I don't know what this is going to lead to, but we're about to find out. He's coming out of the house right now. Look alive."

Bronco had the buttons on his suit shirt mostly undone and the sleeves rolled back. He was angry. He felt like he was ready to blow. He wanted to know how his children could dare betray him in such a manner. He stepped to the brand new Benz and slammed his hand on the hood as hard as he could, leaving a dent. "Both of you, in the fucking house, right now!" he snapped.

Kelly opened the passenger's door and took off running into the mansion. She didn't know what to expect. She had never seen Bronco Banks so furious.

Mills stepped out of the car and closed the door. He sauntered around to the front of it and looked down at the hood. His father had left a small dent the size of a fist right on top of it. He glared at him. "What is your problem?"

"My problem?" Bronco stepped around the car and into his son's face. "If you don't get your ass into the mansion,

I'm going to show you right here in this fucking driveway. Get in there!" he hollered.

Mills looked down at the dent and back to his father. "I don't know what the problem is," he lied. "But this is not okay. You need to learn how to control your anger better." He walked into the mansion, trying to figure out how he was going to weasel his way out of this debacle.

As soon as Bronco stepped inside of the mansion, he slammed the door as hard as he could. "Both you, in the fucking den! Right now!" He stormed behind them, furious. When they made it inside, he watched them take their seats.

Eliza came into the den and took a seat at the table. She set her laptop on the table and refused to make eye contact with anybody inside of the room. She wished she didn't have to be a part of such an event. She was beginning to learn that the Banks family was crazy and full of schemes. As soon as she was able to, she was going to find another more stable job, where there was a sense of normalcy within the work space.

Bronco snapped his fingers at her. "What is that total again?"

Eliza cleared her throat. "Eight hundred thousand, and five hundred dollars."

Bronco eyed his children with deadly anger. "Eight hundred thousand dollars. You ungrateful little pieces of shit, how could you?"

Kelly lowered her head and shook it from side to side. She didn't know what to say. They were caught red-handed. There was no way to ease out of this one, she felt.

"Why am I sitting here with you glaring at me?" Mills asked.

Bronco lowered his eyes. "You and your sister stole over eight hundred thousand dollars from me, and you're going to ask me why you're sitting here? Are you fucking kidding me?"

Mills jumped up. "Eight hundred thousand? What the hell are you talking about? I haven't done no such thing."

Bronco stepped into his face and clenched his jaw. "If you don't sit yo' ass down I'ma beat the shit out you in front of these girls. You been getting by on my kindness for too long. I been sheltering yo' ass. Sit the fuck down, Mills." He clunked his forehead into his, ready to fuck his son over.

Mills's head jerked backward. He felt the stinging pain immediately. It felt like he'd been hit in the head with a bottle. He plopped to the couch reluctantly, mugging his father and rubbing his forehead.

"Now explain to me what would make the two of you rip me off? I give you everything. I rarely say no."

"Dad, it's my fault. Mills didn't have anything to do with it. I've been using the money to try and fund my modeling career. Buying overly expensive clothes and paying my way into expensive places to see if I could make a few connections. I fully intended on paying the money back once I booked a few shoots. I am sorry," Kelly said, keeping her head down.

Mills wanted to speak up, but no words came out of his mouth. He didn't know what to say. He couldn't believe that his sister would bite the bullet in the way that she was. It made him feel some type of way.

Bronco knelt in front of her. "But baby, you're my heart. I would never deny you anything. Why wouldn't you simply come to me so we could work things out for your career? Don't you understand that I want you to succeed as well?"

She nodded. "I do, Dad, but I just couldn't risk you saying no. This modeling is my passion. I want to be the face of a major brand one day. I guess I'm suffering from impatience. I am so sorry, and I swear I'll pay you back every red cent." She placed her face within her hands, and broke down crying. The tears were fake. They were used to soften Bronco.

Bronco sighed and rubbed her back. "Damn. It's okay, baby. Don't beat yourself up about this. I'm angry. I'm disappointed in you, but we'll figure this thing out in another vein. Okay, baby?"

Kelly was in full tears now. Her face was soaked. "Okay, Daddy. I'm so sorry. I'm so sorry. It's just that in Beverly Hills you can't go anywhere without money. You're the laughing stock without droves of cash," she cried.

Bronco pulled her up and into his arms. "Baby girl, it's okay. Daddy got you. I forgive you, baby."

She looked over his shoulder and into Mills's eyes and smiled. Then she snuggled back into Bronco's neck.

***

At eleven o'clock that night, and after the majority of the mansion was asleep, Bronco Banks slipped out of the bed with his wife Jackie and into the north wing. He tiptoed down to Kelly's bedroom. He tapped on the door lightly, turned the knob, and snuck inside.

Kelly laid on her stomach nude under the covers as she was accustomed to sleeping. The night air caused a nice breeze to flow into the room. She slept soundly. Soft jazz played on her radio to help her sleep.

Bronco Banks sat on the bed and ran his big hand over her ass. He squeezed the cheeks after feeling that she was without panties. "Psst, baby girl. Wake up." He dragged his hand into the gap between her thighs and rubbed the sheet into her crease. He could feel the heat from her pussy. It felt hot and meaty.

Kelly inadvertently spread her thighs. She continued to sleep, the feeling of his hand igniting a fire within her belly. Even in the faraway dream she could feel herself getting wet. She moaned deep within her throat.

Bronco had his face in her gap. He licked the sheet after molding it to her box. Her pussy lips formed against it. His tongue flicked up and down her indentation.

Kelly arched her back and spread her thighs as far as she could. She moaned louder, slid her hand under her belly, and opened her sex lips. Her tongue ran all over her lips. Her eyes remained closed. She was still under the spell of sleep.

Bronco stuck his head under the sheet and attacked her bald pussy along with her fingers, which were dripping wet from her juices. Her clitoris stood erect. He teased it, sucked it, and licked up and down her slit. She tasted like sin. Beautiful sin. He couldn't help but to think about the fact that Jackie lay in their marital bed sleeping away while his tongue traced circles around her daughter's clitoris. The thought was overwhelming. He just had to eat and then have her from the back. He had to. It was the only way he could get over the money that she'd ripped him off for. He spread her ass cheeks and licked up and down them. He sucked on her clit from the back, then slipped two fingers into her hole.

"Unnnn!" Kelly was on all fours with her back arched. Her eyes were closed. She licked her pillow. Her pussy juices ran down her thigh.

Bronco lined up his plum head and pushed it into her cat from the back, his dark-skinned penis penetrating her peach lips. She took all ten inches of him. His balls slapped against her clit. He took ahold of her hips and proceeded to plunge in and out of her at full speed.

Her eyes shot open, bringing her into reality. She looked over her shoulder and saw Bronco behind her. Her pussy quivered. She popped her ass back into him as he slammed forward.

Bronco smacked her hard on the ass and pinched her clit before hammering away at her box. "Gimme this pussy, baby girl." Another hard slap on the ass.

"Unh!" She crashed backward over and over. "Unh. Daddy. Daddy. I'm sorry. I'm sorry. Uh! Fuck. Daddy."

Faster and faster. The feeling of her juices leaking off of him was enough to drive him mad. Her pussy felt so good. So tight. So hot. With each stroke it got better and better. He started to groan within his throat, speeding up the pace.

Kelly grabbed her pillow and placed her face into it. She screamed at the top of her lungs. She could feel his piece running in and out of her, elevating her daddy issues. Why did he have to be so big? So wide? Why did his dick feel so good running in and out of her? She slammed backwards into his lap. Bronco had been her first. There had only been three others besides him, and none of them made her cum the way that he did. He was the best. She screamed again and came hard. Shaking. She fell on her stomach with him pounding her out.

Bronco flipped her over and pushed her knees to her chest. He diddled her clitoris with his thumb before slipping back into her furnace. The velvety walls seemed to suck him into her body. She felt so good. He was addicted to her cave. Addicted to her moans. Her scent. Her feel. And he hated it. Hated it because with him, she could get away with murder. He fucked her long and hard, cumming back to back, until he collapsed against her sweaty body. His semen oozed out of her opening along with the evidence of her own multiple orgasms.

Chapter 14

Three weeks later, and after announcing to the city of Los Angeles and the media that he was officially running for mayor, Bronco Banks, sat across the boardroom table and looked into the eyes of his campaign chairman. His name was Russell Rose. He was Jewish, an investment banker and corporate attorney. He was 5'6" tall, balding at the top of his head. He kept his face clean-shaven. He was soft spoken and cunning. He tapped away at his laptop and spun it around so Bronco could see the face of Dwayne Haynes.

"This is going to be your stiffest competition, Mr. Banks. According to the numbers, he is ahead if you by eighteen points in the mayoral race, and projected to be the winner if the race was to end today."

"Dwayne? How is that possible? Where is all of his support stemming from?" Bronco wanted to know.

"Apparently the Crenshaw District."

"My district?"

"Yes. He is spear heading the Stop the Violence movement. Ever since he's started that campaign, crime has been down by forty percent in the Crenshaw district. He was born and raised in Baldwin Village. He attended Crenshaw High school on Eleventh Avenue and is a pastor at the West Angeles Church of God and Christ right in the heart of Crenshaw on Exposition Boulevard. He is deeply-rooted within the community over there, and as long as the violence numbers continue to go south, he's going to be a sure pick for the mayoral seat. I'm sorry, sir."

Bronco's brain was having a hard time processing this. "Is there any way to help me in the polls? We need this seat, Russell. It's the only way that Banks Properties can extend across California and we can make some real political connections. It's not what you know, it's who you know. You do understand that, right?"

"Of course I do, sir."

"Well then, what do we do?" Bronco snapped.

Russell gazed over at Eliza. He cleared his throat. "Sir, may I speak freely, or should we wait to discuss this matter until your accountant isn't in the room?"

Bronco waved him off. "I trust Eliza. She's a good girl. Loyal. You may speak freely."

Eliza blushed and lowered her head. She continued breaking down the numbers for his real estate developing company. The quarter had come to an end, and he needed the totals to file his taxes.

Russell got up and closed the door. He lowered the blinds of the office and exhaled loudly. "Sir, apparently Dwayne is winning over that district by stopping the violence, and he's supposed to be purchasing a few buildings from the city so that he can turn them into YMCA's, and Boys and Girls clubs. He's been ridding the streets of crime in that area. Sir, the only way for us to knock him out of the box would be to reverse everything that he is doing."

Bronco was facing the window and looking up to the few clouds that were in the sky. It took a second for what Russell had spoken to sink in with him. "So what exactly are you saying, Russell?"

Russell loosened his tie. "Listen, sir, with all due respect, if you are looking to win this election, you're going to have to okay dirty politics. After all, this is Los Angeles."

Bronco Banks paused and nodded. "Go on."

"We're going to have to figure out a way to raise the crime rate in that area. Also, the buildings that he's looking to purchase are still on the market. We'll buy those, and use them as a campaign catapult. There is someone that I am connected with that has an influential position within his circle. They're about the numbers. A simple pay off for inside information oughta do it. We'll stay one step ahead at all times. Beat him to the punch with everything, and we'll make him break every promise he intends to keep. It's simple. In a matter of weeks, we ought to see your numbers rise, and his begin to dwindle. First things first. We need a corrupter from the community that will know how to break down the community. Someone that will work for cash. You have anybody in mind?" he asked.

Bronco sighed and took a seat at the head of the table. He knew just where to go. It would hurt his heart to do such, and he didn't know how he was going to be received, but he definitely knew where to go. "Yeah, I know somebody."

***

Cheyenne pulled her red Dodge Stratus to the curb and parked it. She blew the horn three times to get her mother's attention. She'd just finished grocery shopping. The car was full of grocery bags, and so was the trunk. She got out and popped the trunk. Then she noticed that there was a black Jaguar parked two cars up from her own in front of one of her older neighbor's single story houses. She scanned the neighborhood. It seemed as if it was a normal, hot day in Crenshaw. Most of the people on the block were having water fights with balloons, squirt guns, and buckets of water. There were a bunch of dope boys washing their fresh rides and getting prepared for the day. They seemed oblivious to her and the Jaguar, which she knew couldn't have belonged to the old lady whose house it was parked in front of. She shrugged her shoulders and carried the first couple bags up to the house. The main door was wide open, but the screen door was locked. She could smell reefer. She heard the sounds of Earth, Wind, and Fire serenading out of the speakers. She pounded on the screen door. "Mama, open the door."

Sondra came to the door laughing. Her eyes were lower than a midget's ankles. "Aw, hey baby, bring yo' li'l self on in. Your father's here." She held the door open for her to walk into the house.

Cheyenne gasped. "My what?"

Sondra's smile turned upside down. "Baby, please don't make a big thing of this. He comes bearing gifts. He missed us. Just come on in, and play it cool," she ordered her daughter.

Cheyenne felt instantly offended. How dare her mother tell her to play it cool when she had so many things to be upset about? Her father was filthy rich with millions of dollars, and yet they stayed in a single story duplex. Every month they panicked because they didn't know how they were going to come up with money for the bills, and on the other side of town, somewhere in Bel Air, her father Bronco Banks had a whole other family that he spoiled to death. It wasn't fair. So it was going to be hard to be cool. She carried the bags into the living room and set them on the floor.

When Bronco saw his daughter, he stood up with and set the shot of VSOP on the table. She was just as beautiful as the last time he'd seen her. "Cheyenne, baby, you look amazing." He opened his arms for her to step into them.

Cheyenne mugged him and rolled her eyes. "What do you want, Bronco? The only time you show up is when you're up to something. So what's good?"

Bronco took a step back, offended. "Baby, what have I done to hurt you?" He was oblivious. There was nothing that Cheyenne could ask of him that he wouldn't do for her. It had always been that way.

"I ain't got nothing to say to you, old man. How about you go out there and carry the rest of those bags into the house? My feet hurt." She rolled her eyes again and left him standing looking like a damn fool in the living room.

Sondra set two bags on the floor and looked over to him. She could tell that he was hurt, and maybe even on the verge of tears. As much as he had taken her through, she still held a soft spot in her heart for him. "Hey, Bronco, don't mind her. She's just feeling the pains from our broken relationship. We go through a lot here as a family on a daily basis. The fact that we're still living in the ghetto, and you're living in the lap of luxury, is still a hard pill to swallow."

"But Sondra, I'll give you guys anything that I have. You know that. To see my baby girl act like that towards me breaks my heart," he admitted.

Noodles stepped into the house with arms full of groceries. Filipino was right behind him with the same amount. When Noodles saw Bronco Banks he stopped in his tracks and set the bags on the floor. "Mama, what the fuck is this clown doing here?" he asked, mugging Bronco.

"Hey, Noodles, watch your mouth, son!" Sondra chastised.

Noodles moved her behind him. He stepped into Bronco's face. "'Sup, cuz? You think you finna get between my mama thighs, you got another thang coming, potna. That shit ain't happening."

Cheyenne stepped into the living room. "Holy shit, Noodles." She knew she had to get in there and in between the men. Noodles hated their father's guts, especially after what Bronco had done to her.

Bronco swallowed. "Nadell, why is it that every time we come into contact, we have to wind up here? When will we let bygones be bygones?"

"When you resting peace for how you treated my moms and for what you did to my sister. No justice no peace, homie, and I'm so close to giving yo' ass some justice that peace can't be that far behind."

"Say, Cuz, I'ma wait for you outside, Noodles," Filipino announced. He already knew how he was. If he thought that Noodles was about to handle some bidness with his old man, he would assist him. That's just how they rolled, and they didn't give a fuck who had something to say about it.

"Cool, Cuz," he returned to Filipino. He looked into Bronco's eyes and stared. "What brings you to the hood, old man?"

Bronco was trying his best to hold his composure. "I wanted to see my family. I missed y'all. That and I need to have a sit down with you."

"With me? What for?" Noodles clenched his jaw off and on. He felt his blood pressure rising. He was strapped with two Glock Forties, and he felt like emptying both clips into his old man. The sight of Bronco Banks disgusted him.

"We just need to talk business that's all. Man stuff. You know, out of earshot of your mother and sister." He looked from Cheyenne to Sondra.

Noodles scoffed. "These my people. Anything you gotta say to me, you can say in front of them, and if you can't, then you can step the fuck off. Ain't nothing you gon' offer me gon' stop me from wanting to use one of these on yo' ass, Cuz." He pulled both Glocks from the small of his back.

Bronco backed away and held his hands in the air. "Say, Nadell, come on now."

Noodles raised both guns and cocked the hammers. "You's a bitch nigga, Pops, on everythang, Cuz. Tell me something to stop me from putting four holes in your face."

"Noodles, please," Sondra pleaded. She didn't want to see her son kill his father. She knew how much hatred he held in his heart for the man. She knew that he craved killing him after he'd caught him doing what he had to Cheyenne. "Please, son."

Cheyenne felt a tingle go down her spine. She looked on with mounting interest. She didn't know if she wanted Noodles to pull the trigger or for her mother to break the whole thing up. She loved her brother. He was her heart. She didn't want to see him lose his life, but at the same time, their father was a low life scumbag. He probably deserved a bullet.

"What you think, Cheyenne? It's your call, sis. You tell me to waste this clown for what he did to you and we'll vacuum his brains from the carpet later as a family. It's your call, dead, or alive?"

Bronco was shaking. His knees knocked. He didn't know how his son had become so crazy. There was no light in his eyes. He looked like a possessed demon. "Nadell, son. You don't have to do this. I am your father."

"What's it gon' be, Cheyenne? This nigga dead or alive?" Noodles asked, sliding his fingers around the triggers.

Cheyenne didn't know what to say. Sweat creased her brow. She felt her stomach turning over. She bit into her bottom lip.

"What's good, sis?" Noodles yelled.

"Cheyenne, please?" Bronco pleaded.

"Tell him to put it down, baby. Please, Cheyenne. Do it for, Mama."

"Don't play her, Mama. It's her call. He hurt her more than the both of us. What's good, sis?"

Cheyenne grabbed her face. She felt like she was about to have a nervous breakdown. She saw what it looked like for Noodles to pull the trigger, and it was overwhelming. She fainted and dropped to the floor.

Noodles placed both guns into the small of his back and rushed to Cheyenne's side, taking her into his arms. "Cheyenne? Cheyenne?" He kissed her cheek and brushed her hair out of her face.

Bronco took the distraction as a chance to get the hell out of the living room. He rushed outside and down the stairs. He slipped on the first two and tumbled down the last four.

Filipino was sitting on the hood of his car, smoking a blunt of Maui. When he saw Bronco, he jumped off of it. He thought about upping his toolie. He didn't know what the heck was going on. "Say, what up, cuz?"

Bronco stood up and dusted off his pants. He jogged to Filipino and pulled out his card. "I don't know is the matter with my son, but you take this number and give me a call if you want to make some serious cash. I'm talking hundreds of thousands of dollars. You hear me?"

Filipino snatched the card and mugged him. "What I gotta do, Cuz? It bet' not be nothing toward the homie. I'll murder you for asking me some shit like that." Filipino felt himself becoming heated.

Bronco chirped the alarm of his Jaguar. "I love my son. I would never hurt him. You just hit me up. I promise to change the both of your lives. I'm set to be the mayor of this town. Here, give this to my family." He threw him a huge knot of hundred dollar bills totaling fifty thousand, then jumped into his car and stormed away from the curb.

Filipino looked over the knot. He noticed that a bunch of people from the neighborhood were looking him over closely as he thumbed through the money. He snapped and pulled out a 45. "Fuck y'all looking at?! Huh? Mafuckas got a problem?" He aimed his gun in the air and let off five shots. That cleared the neighborhood.

Hood Rich

Chapter 15

Fancii waited patiently on the couch in the waiting room of Covergirl. Out of the ten models that had auditioned for the cosmetic line, she had been the sixth. That had been an hour ago, and she couldn't think straight ever since then. She was praying that she booked the job. The pay was fifteen grand, and her commercial would run for three months. If she could get this job, it would open up so many doors. She could only imagine where the platform could take her. She stood up and paced back and forth in the waiting area. The sight of so many beautiful women was enough to cause her self-esteem to waver. They came in all colors and creeds. The competition was staggering. She'd been holding in a full tank of pee for over an hour. Finally, after not being able to take it anymore, she rushed to the bathroom, pulled a covering over the toilet, and sat down, peeing like the wind. After she finished, she washed her hands and looked into the mirror. "You are beautiful. You are rare. You can do this. You will be an asset to this company. Love you."

A toilet flushed and a tall Brazilian stepped out of a stall with a smirk on her face. "That's your pep talk, huh? You gon' need to say and believe more than that to survive in this business." She brushed past her and set her Birkin makeup bag on the counter. "Besides, you're too short for Covergirl. You're built more for Sears, or JCPenney," she quipped, trying her best to knock Fancii's self-esteem down a few pegs.

"Um, excuse you, but do you know me?" Fancii asked, drying her hands with a paper towel.

The Brazilian smiled and continued to apply her lipstick. "Girl, I don't need to know you. I see females like you come through these doors all the time. They have high hopes and dreams. They aspire to be something great, not knowing that this business is designed to eat you alive. The people in it will use and abuse you. Then when they are tired of you, or they feel like replacing you, you're gone without so much as a greeting card. If you're already giving yourself pep talks, then you don't stand a chance. You're weak." She curled her lip and gave Fancii a look of disgust.

Fancii stepped next to her and slammed her hand on the vanity style sink. She felt offended and highly disrespected. "Listen to me, bitch. I don't know who you are, or who the fuck you think you are, but you don't know nothing about me, or my strength. I come from nothing. The gutter. I wake up every morning with one thing on my mind: success. I live in a household where I am basically the only reliable provider and it's been that way ever since I was fifteen years old. I've overcome starvation, gang violence, drive-by shootings, mental and physical abuse, and most recently the murder of somebody close to me. So don't you tell me what I'm not strong enough to endure. On top of all of that, I am a woman. Fearless. Now check your attitude, and your judging. You are not Jehovah. You do not have the last and final say so."

The Brazilian looked dumbfounded. She didn't know what to say. She wanted to apologize to Fancii, but it seemed too late for that. Her response had blindsided her completely. The first thing she'd noticed about Fancii was her unmistakable beauty. She saw her as visual competition. She felt that if she could throw a few slugs at her, it would lower her self-esteem and cause her to flee.

A toilet flushed and Marsha Brads, the chief editor for the fashion magazine section of Covergirl stepped out of a stall. She stepped next to Fancii and washed her hands. She was white, six feet tall, slim, and absolutely gorgeous. She looked to be in her early forties. She exuded power and prestige. "You're going to be great in this business, young Queen. Just you watch." She took two paper towels and dried her hands. She eyed the Brazilian and shook her head before leaving the bathroom.

Fancii felt like she wanted to throw up. She wished she had known that Marsha Brads had been inside of the bathroom. She would have never acted so offensively toward the Brazilian. Damn, something had told her to bit her tongue. Now she feared the worst.

The Brazilian swallowed her spit. She placed all of her cosmetics back into her makeup bag. "I apologize, and seriously, I wish you the best. You are truly beautiful." She opened the door to the bathroom and left.

Fancii took a deep breath and eyed herself in the mirror again. "You're okay, God got you, girl. Keep fighting." She exhaled loudly one more time and left the bathroom.

***

"So basically that means that if your father doesn't capture south Los Angeles, most importantly the Crenshaw District, he is going to lose this election. According to the polls, Mayor Haynes has a strong following amongst minorities in this district, which is a little weird because your father is an alderman in Baldwin Village." Eliza exhaled. "He has to turn things around quick, or you can forget about moving into the governor's mansion."

Mills eyed the laptop closely and balled his fist before slamming it on the table and standing up. "Fuck, it's always something." He paced back and forth. There were a million thoughts running through his head that were driving him crazy. There was no way he could allow his father to lose

the election. The mayor's seat meant power. It meant political connections. He would be able to link with the power
heads in other states. His father would be guaranteed four
years as the mayor during which time Mills would cease
every moment to benefit himself. He had plans to open strip
clubs and dispensaries all over the state of California. It
would give him a reason for not going to college. He hated
school more than anything else in the world. "So what do
you think has to happen?"

Eliza got up and gave him a card. "You need to call this
number and set up a meeting with this thug. His name is
Antwan Roberts, but the streets refer to him as Combo. He
is a dominant force within the streets of South Los Angeles.
You're gonna wanna tell him to turn up the violence at
every turn, and you're going to want to supply him with
everything that he needs to destroy that area. The more destruction, the higher the poll numbers rise for your father,
and they will fall for Mr. Haynes. It's as simple as that."

Mills Googled Combo and scrolled down the long log
of his rap sheet. He gathered right away that Combo wasn't
going to be somebody to play with. The sight of the thug's
rap sheet and physical features made him nervous. "So
what do I do, call him or something? Is he expecting the
call?"

Eliza nodded. "Honestly, I've taken it upon myself to
set a meeting for the two of you. You're going to be meeting him in three hours at a restaurant in Baldwin Hills. He
knows who you are, and that this meeting is of extreme im-
portance. Now look, we have a budget of twenty thousand
a week, but he will not get the first payment until we see
there has been some sort of uproar in the community. Your
father is behind by eleven points right now. There has to be
a major turn around, and soon. This guy is the key."

Mills continued to look over the screen. He felt uncomfortable parading around in the ghetto. But since it was for the greater good of his family and his position in life, he would have to grin and bear it. "A'ight, make sure that I have some form of security detail and I'll be ready to roll out in an hour."

Eliza nodded. "I'm already on it. Two men, ex-police officers. Trained in the streets. You're good."

Mills frowned. "It seems like you've become more than an accountant for my father. What do you have up your sleeve?" he asked, circling around her chair.

She felt nervous. Her confidence wavered. "I just want your father to be as successful as he possibly can, you know, since I'm coming along for the ride and everything." Eliza craved success. She wanted to exceed her parents' expectations. If she could get into the mayor's mansion, it could open up the field for her politically. She could be the youngest cabinet member to ever step foot in the Capitol Building. The thought made her feel breathless for a moment.

Mills smiled and ran his hand along her shoulder. "Oh, okay. So I'm not the only one that is looking to ride my father's success to a much better position in life. It seems that we all have our hidden agendas?"

Eliza stood up and faced him. "I don't have any hidden agenda. My agenda is well known. I am willing to work hard to get to where I need to be in life. Your father has provided me a ship to use as a vessel to navigate opportunities. I am going to use each one that I come across because I want so much out of life, and I am looking to obtain a lot of those things by the time I reach the age of thirty. If you have a problem with that, I don't know what to tell you."

Mills laughed. He stepped into her face. "Oh, now who is this new Barbie, might I ask? It seems that we've found ourselves a supple amount of courage. Kudos." He stepped into her face even more.

Eliza took a step back in the den. She suddenly felt uncomfortable. She hated being alone with him because things never went how they were supposed to. She wished that he was a better businessman and opportunist. If he would get his head out of his ass, he could have seen that Bronco Banks becoming mayor of California meant limitless possibilities for all of those that were involved with him. What they did leading up to and during his term was going to be important for the betterment of their futures. "Mills, why don't you save this macho card that you're playing with me for Antwan? I'm on your side. I am sure that we both want the same things. Besides, this act is becoming a tad bit tired. Your birthday is coming soon. It's time you become a man." She made a move to step around him.

This offended Mills. He grabbed her by her Prada suit coat and slammed her against the wall, causing the laptop to fall off of the table. He hemmed her up. "Bitch, you listen to me real carefully. I brought you into my family's structure. I gave you this position. You are here because of me. Now I don't give a fuck how cozy you are getting with my father. You work for me. You got that?"

She nodded. Her suit coat was up around her neck, cutting off her air supply. "Yes. Yes. I'm sorry," she choked out.

Mills released her and straightened out her jacket. "Now that's better." He rubbed her cheek with his fingers. "You and I have the same goals, baby. We are both looking to capitalize off of my old man. I say we do it together. You feel me?"

Eliza's heart was pounding in her chest. She would tell him anything to get him the hell out of there. "Yes. I feel you."

Mills leaned forward and kissed her soft lips, ran his tongue across them. He sucked the top one, and then the bottom one into his mouth. "It's me and you, baby. Ride or die. Bonnie and Clyde. Am I right?"

Eliza began to shake like a leaf. "Right."

"Right," he repeated.

He pulled her skirt above her hips and pressed her more firmly against the wall. He unbuckled his belt and dropped his pants just enough. He spread her legs and entered into her hot pussy with one stroke.

"Uh. Mills," Eliza moaned before he picked her up. She wrapped her legs around him.

Mills bounced her up and down on his pipe. She was hot and wet. Tighter than he remembered. Her insides were slippery. He could feel her breath panting along his right cheek.

She dug her nails into his shoulder blades, bouncing up and down, his dick stretching her wide. "Mills. Mills. Oooh. Please don't. Unh. Unh."

"Say. It's. Me. And. You. Say. It," he ordered, bouncing her up and down. The pussy got better and better with each stroke.

He hit her G-spot over and over. "It's. Us. It's. Us. Awwww. Please. Mills!" She bounced with her back rubbing up and down against the wall. She couldn't believe he was fucking her like this. Exploiting his authority over her. It was demoralizing.

He carried her to the desk, spread her legs wide, and commenced to pounding her out at full speed, going as deep as his dick would allow him to. Both of her ankles were on his shoulders. The backs of her thighs were against his chest. That pussy was good to him. "It's us, Eliza. It's us. You. Hear. Me?" Harder and harder.

Eliza threw her head back and moaned deep within her throat. She grabbed him around the neck and came harder than she ever had in her entire life. She was still shaking like crazy when he bent her over and started to fuck her as hard as he could from the back.

Mills knew that she worked closely with his father. If he was going to keep tabs on the old man, he had to conquer her, and that's what he intended to do.

Chapter 16

Whoom! Filipino kicked in the front door and stepped to the side. Noodles ran inside the house with two Forty Glocks cocked and loaded.

The first thing he saw was a table with three dudes seated at it. They were aluminum foiling large quantities of China White. When they heard the knocking in of the front door, instead of getting up and running for their lives, they remained seated at the table, frozen in place. All three were higher than they should have been.

Noodles rushed to the dude closest to him, and smacked him with the banger, knocking him to the floor. He aimed his gun at the other two. "Get the fuck on the ground right now or it's finna be a muthafuckin' murder scene off in this bitch," he promised.

They dropped to the floor. Both men were stuck, caught off-guard. They wondered what was set to happen next. Noodles ran his hands all over them, recovering their guns and putting them on his hip. "Check the crib, bruh."

Filipino was already on it. He kicked open one door after the next. He searched inside the rooms, finding no other person. It smelled of crack cocaine and funk all through the house, which was ironic because the dudes were in there putting together heroin. He wondered why that was, but didn't want to place too much on it. After checking the house from top to bottom and making sure that no one else was present, he rushed back into the living room.

Noodles was dumping the bricks of China White into his garbage bag. "Where is the money? Where the fuck is the money at?" he hollered. He kicked one of the men in the ass.

"I don't know. I don't know. I swear to God I don't," the dark-skinned man yelled.

Filipino took a pillow off of the couch and stood over him. He aimed his gun at the man's face. He'd been given his orders. Whether they cooperated or not, he was going to smoke everybody in the house and make sure it got on the news. He had to make sure that bodies began to drop so that it would work against Mayor Haynes's campaign. Bronco Banks had made things very clear. "Where the money at, li'l nigga? This your last chance."

"Man, I just started working here two days ago. I ain't in charge of the money. He is." He nodded his head at the first dude that Noodles had smacked with the gun.

"Yeah, well, I'ma ask him next." He stuffed the pillow over his face and pulled the trigger twice. The gun burned two holes into the pillow. The scent of burnt cloth and gunpowder drifted into the air.

Noodles jumped back. He was confused. He wanted to question Filipino's motives, but knew that in the middle of a job was always the wrong time to do that. Instead, he snatched up the first dude and put his gun to his forehead. "Where the money at, cuz? As you can see, we ain't on no bullshit here. Ain't no sense in you dying for another nigga's money. We already got the bricks. Where dat cash at?"

The dude's eyes rolled into the back of his head. Blood oozed out of his wound and slid down his face in thick rivers. "In the couch, way on the bottom. Its fifteen G's right now. Combo was supposed to come and pick it up in an hour. He gon' be mad to find it gone."

Noodles smacked him. "Which couch, homie? The love seat, or the ottoman?"

142

He spit blood across the carpet and pointed to the ottoman.

Filipino snatched up the remaining dude and flung him over to the ottoman. "Grab that money out, cuz. Throw that shit right on the floor stack by stack. Hurry up, before you rest in peace wit' ya homeboy right there."

The dude dug his arm into the couch and pulled out the money that he was just ordered to place into it not more than ten minutes before Noodles and Filipino had kicked in the door. He threw stack after stack on to the floor until there was nothing left. It totaled just over fifteen thousand dollars.

Filipino pulled a pillow case out of his waistband and dumped the money inside of it. It looked like twice as much as fifteen thousand because it was mostly in ones and five dollar bills. Once he placed all of the cash in there, he grabbed the dude up by his dreadlocks. "Say, potna, where the rest of these bricks at?"

He shook his head. "This all I know about. Combo don't tell me shit, bruh. That's straight up."

Filipino wasn't trying to hear that. In that moment, he was looking for any reason to smoke the dude anyway. He figured that three dead bodies in a house would make the five, six, and ten o'clock news, and cause a splash. He flipped his gun on safety, and slammed the barrel into the dudes head as hard as he could. He knocked him backward. When he fell to the floor Filipino straddled him and beat him into a bloody pulp. When he stood up, he could see that the dude was no longer breathing. He lay on his back with his eyes wide open, and blood spilling out everywhere. "Fuck, nigga. This shit ain't a game."

Noodles frowned under his mask. Now he was really confused. He didn't get why Filipino had done what he had.

"Bruh, you tripping. That nigga couldn't have known shit. It's clear Combo fucks with this clown right here, and the other two was regular workers."

Filipino shrugged his shoulders. "Fuck these niggas. We ain't got room to be playing with these suckas, man. We gotta get ours and turn all the way up." He extended his gun to the dude that Noodles was holding. "Where the rest of them bricks at, nigga? Huh?"

The dude's head had swelled. It looked like a pumpkin, and it was getting more and more swollen by the minute. "There is a bed in the back room. Throw the mattress off the top of it, and search inside of the box spring. There is two more bricks of China in there." He closed his eyes and swallowed his blood.

Noodles nodded at Filipino.

Filipino jogged out of the living room and into the backroom. He rushed inside and tossed the mattress off of it. He spotted the box spring. He flipped it over and proceeded to search it thoroughly before coming across the packages. His eyes lit up. "Oh, hell yeah. This what the fuck I'm talking about." He stuffed the bricks into his bag and ran out of the room. "I got 'em. Let's bounce, Cuz, fuck this nigga." He bumped Noodles just enough to move him out of the way, extended his arm, and shot the remaining dude twice right through his forehead. His brains jumped out of the back of his head and wound up on the carpet behind him. Filipino stepped over of him and grabbed his bag of spoils. "Let's get the fuck out of here, Cuz." He ran out the back door and to the car they'd parked in the alley.

Noodles looked around the crime scene. There were three dead bodies. All of them were left in a horrible state. Before the lick, he was sure that get wouldn't have had to kill anybody, and he still felt that those murders were un-necessary. Something wasn't right with Filipino, and he had to get to the bottom of it real soon. He looked over the crime scene one last time and shook his head before run-ning behind his right hand man.

***

Mills slid into the booth of Mabel's Homestyle Chicken and Waffles. Combo was already seated at the booth with a scowl on his face. He had men in position all around the restaurant. They were heavily armed, and ready for the un-known. The two security guards that were in charge to pro-tect Mills sat two tables over. Their guns had been stripped from them at the door. They felt uneasy. They'd done their research on Combo. He was vicious and what they deemed as an evader. They knew that he orchestrated a bunch of crimes, but he had a way of distancing himself far enough so that nothing ever came back to him. Both men were sweating in the uncomfortable environment.

Mills had popped two Percocets. He was feeling breezy. He knew he had to handle the thug like he knew what he was doing. He summoned all of the strength deep within the pits of his heart and looked into Combo's red eyes. "So you're supposed to be the man down here, huh?"

Combo scoffed. "That's the reason they sent you my way, ain't it?" He didn't like this pretty boy muthafucka. Everything was too perfect about him - even his finger-nails. He'd already caught sight of his nails when Mills had first taken his seat in front of him. They looked freshly manicured. That made him laugh.

Mills looked into his ugly face. "Check this out, bro."

"I'm not yo muthafuckin' bro. This here is bidness only. All my brothers live to die in L.A. with me. Let's get that shit straight right now." He took a vial of China White out of his inside coat pocket, poured a substantial amount on the table, and tooted two lines. The drug attacked his brain and caused his senses to heighten. He felt numb. Relaxed. Ready to talk business. And also murderous. "Say, rich kid, all you gotta do is explain to me what you need for me to do and we'll go from there. You better speak up, though, because once that sun goes all the way down, Crenshaw becomes the belly of the beast. That Benz you rolling out there will be donated to the cause. Not even I can stop that shit from happening." Combo laughed.

Mills felt a chill go down his spine. He glanced out of the window. Not only was it getting darker, but there was a group of dudes standing across the street mugging his new Benz. He felt that he had to get an understanding with Combo and get the hell out of there. He swallowed his spit and tried to calm down. "Well, it's quite simple what I need. I need for you to turn the Crenshaw community upside down. We need for the crime rate to increase significantly. Now I won't micromanage what you do, exactly, just as long as we see some results."

"How much am I getting paid, and when will I see the first portion of my money?" Combo interrupted.

"Twenty grand a week, and you'll see the first payment as soon as you get started. That sound like a plan?" Mils asked.

Combo sucked his teeth. "N'all, fuck that. I want my money up front. This is the ghetto. Money on the wood makes the deal all good. Run me my cheese, and we'll go from there. It's as simple as that."

Mills was growing impatient. He had visions of spitting directly into Combo's face. He couldn't believe that he thought that he actually was somebody. In Mills's opinion, he was nothing more than a lowlife scum bag. A send-off. An inevitable body in the morgue. It was hard for him to not tell him everything that he thought. He had to keep his father's campaign at the forefront of his brain, as well as the fact that his life hung in the balance. "Well, I will get back to my people, and I will let you know what's what then." He stood up.

Combo mugged him. "Nigga, sit yo' punk ass back down. You don't end this meeting until I say you can leave. This ain't Beverly Hills, boy. This is Crenshaw. I run this shit." He clenched his jaw and mugged Mills with hatred.

Mills reluctantly took a seat. "What's the problem?" He sighed.

"The problem is your attitude. I'ma need you to fix that muthafucka, or you gon' find your head lying beside your body, playboy. You don't mean shit to me. You or your punk ass daddy. All I care about is my money. Thirty G's, every Monday. I will cause chaos from Monday until Sunday. Monday you will pay me again, and so forth and so on. The minute you stop paying me, we got a problem. Point blank period." He looked at his Rolex watch. "It's seven o'clock. Today is Sunday. I expect you to have my first payment by tomorrow morning. Have it, and we'll go from there. You're dismissed."

Chapter 17

After two weeks of hitting a selective few of Combo's trap houses, Noodles was at a grand total of thirty thousand dollars. He felt good. He felt that he and Filipino were making headway. The money would help him to continue to pay his mother's and sister's bills. The trickle down that was left over would help him to get himself together for the most part. He had been stuck wearing the same four outfits for so long that it had become normal to him. Now that he had the money he could purchase himself some new clothes and shoes. The next caper was supposed to be big. It would allow him to stack some major chips. The goal was to accrue enough money so he could move his mother and sister out of the ghetto and into a nice portion of the suburbs.

But it wasn't going to be easy. The streets seemed to be turning fouler by the day, and Filipino acted as if he was flying off of the handle. In just over two weeks' time, he'd smoked at least nine people. Noodles had smoked four, and that was only because they wouldn't give up what they had without a fight. The Game was getting darker for Noodles. He knew he couldn't remain in it forever without getting either locked up or murdered in the streets. Either outcome would shatter his mother.

It was eight o'clock in the evening on a rainy day, and he was missing Fancii like crazy. He hadn't seen her in a full week, and he needed to. He was thinking about all of this as he stepped up her stairs and knocked on the door. It seemed that the rain picked up behind him. He waited a few moments, and then knocked again.

Fancii opened the main door and peered at him through the screen. She had her long hair pulled back over her shoulder in a ponytail. She wore a pair of white pajamas that she'd worn ever since she was fourteen years old. Though they were snug in the backside, for the most part they still fit her quite comfortably. "Noodles." She opened the door and allowed him to come inside.

Noodles stomped his feet on the welcome mat and dragged them over it a few times before stepping into the house. He waited until she closed the door, and then snatched her into his strong arms and hugged her for a full minute. Then they were passionately making out.

Fancii wrapped her arms around his neck and continued to invade his mouth with her smaller tongue. She moaned and felt his big hands all over her ass, squeezing her soft hefty cheeks. She thought about her mother being in the other room and broke their affection by taking a step back. Her heart was beating hard in her chest. "Noodles, we gotta chill. My mother just laid down because of a migraine but I don't want her to pop up and catch us in a full-on make out session. That would be kind of awkward." She ran her thumb over his lips to remove some of her spit. "What brings you over here tonight anyway?"

Noodles felt offended. "Damn, I gotta have a reason to wanna come out and see my woman now? Can't I just miss you in the way that I'm supposed to?"

Fancii locked the door and sat down on the couch. "Noodles, you ain't been to see me in an entire week. It's clear that you don't be missing me like that because if you did, there is no way that you could stand to be away from me as much as you do. In fact, your distance has got me to thinking some crazy thoughts."

Noodles didn't like the sound of that. Fancii was the love of his life. He was one hunnid to her, and always had been. She was the only female that he'd ever been with that he'd never cheated on. That's not to say that the thought hadn't crossed his mind because the females in Los Angeles at times put on the pressure, but he respected her too much. He loved her, and couldn't ever see himself hurting her on purpose. He sat beside her in the leather couch. It made crunching sounds because Fancii's mother kept the plastic on it all year round. "What type of thinking you been doing, baby?"

Fancii sighed. "I've just been thinking that maybe you and I are going down two separate paths. I think that right now is a time for us to be focused on what we want to achieve out of life. I want more than this." She waved her hand through the air. "And in order for me to get it, I'm going to have to bust my ass every second of every day. My family is on my back. That's a lot of pressure."

Noodles was silent. He understood what she was saying. He'd heard those same words from her ever since they were sixteen years old. While he understood it, he couldn't help but to feel like she was slapping him in the face every time she said it now, as if she saw herself going places and him remaining stagnant. It was a bit insulting and bruising to his ego. "Baby, I thought that we were going to find our way out of this ghetto together. Whatever happened to that?"

Fancii shrugged her shoulders. "I don't know. I guess it just seems to me that nothing is really changed with you. You're still doing the exact same things that you were two years ago, or even as recent as last spring. You're expecting a different result, but you're demonstrating the same behaviors, baby. That's a sign of insanity. I'm just tired, Noodles."

Noodles hopped up. He felt himself becoming angry. "Damn, Fancii." He dug five grand out of his pocket. The money was encased in a rubber band. He dropped it on the glass table. "That is for you, baby. I am doing the best that I absolutely can. I'm out there busting my ass in these streets every single day to make a way for the both of our families. It's not about me. It's about y'all. I wanna get my mother out of the ghetto, first and foremost. Then I wanna make sure that you escape this bullshit too. I wanna support your dreams and stand behind you as your man, while at the same time chasing my own. Baby, I've been so consumed with trying to make things happen for everybody else that I don't even know what I want out of life for myself. Damn."

Fancii stood up. There was the loud sound of a helicopter traveling past in the sky. It sounded as if it was actually inside of the living room with them. "And that's a problem, baby. It's a problem if you're trying to do so much and you're losing yourself in the process. That's not how life works," she assured him.

"Yeah, well, for me it does. I been doing what I had to do ever since I was old enough to know that my father wasn't shit. That he was a deadbeat and that my family didn't mean shit to him. I been paying the bills since I was fourteen years old. Month after month, year after year. So when you talk about having your family on your back, I know a little bit about that." He shook his head.

Fancii stepped over to him, and tried to rest her hand on his shoulder. She could tell that he was upset. She wanted to comfort him. To calm him down. "Noodles, can we sit down and talk for a minute?"

He jerked away from her. "Talk about what, Fancii? Clearly you got something on your mind that ain't right, so why don't you just spit it out, and we'll stop playing these games. Are you saying you wanna break up?"

Fancii was shocked that he would even ask such a thing. She didn't think that she'd let on that much, but Mills was heavy in the back of her brain. He'd already purchased her a condo and paid up the rent for six months. Fancii couldn't allow herself to move into it while still being linked to Noodles. She felt that would have been so dirty. Her conscience would have never allowed her to. "Noodles, I don't know if I was thinking anything as extreme as that. I was just wondering if maybe we needed a break or something. Not a permanent one, just a breather to do some thinking so we can get our lives on track. Right now I'm so confused about everything that I don't know what to. It's crazy."

Noodles couldn't believe his ears. He stood there frozen in time and silence. After everything that was going on, the one person who he knew for sure would always be by his side sounded as if she was abandoning him. "Who is this other nigga, Fancii?"

She almost choked on her spit. Her heart dropped into her stomach. "What?"

"You heard me. Who is this nigga that got your attention? Don't say nobody because for you to be kicking me to the curb you gotta have somebody else in mind that you feel is worthy of taking my place. Now who the fuck is he?"

Fancii started to bite on the nail of her index finger. There was no way she was going to tell Noodles about Mills. She feared that he would track him down and take his life with no hesitation. Noodles was crazy about her and she knew it. No, she couldn't place Noodles on Mills's trail. That would be a death sentence for him. "Noodles, this has nothing to do with another man. This is about us getting our lives on track. Securing our futures before we come together to build what we can for each other. We're both unstable. What can we possibly offer one another?"

Noodles felt his heart being ripped out of him. He couldn't believe how she was talking. This was his sweetheart. The young love of his life. His rib. He stared to imagine what life would be like without her and it made him sick to his stomach. He'd once felt that Fancii was the only stability he had in his life. Now with her fading away, he felt broken in a sense. "You know what, Fancii? I love you, shawty. I don't know what's going on with you, but I swear to God I love you, and no matter what, I'ma keep fighting for us and our future. I am going to be the one to get us out of this hood. Not just you and I, but our families as a whole. I know it deep down in my soul that I am. It's finna be hard, but I got this. I got them, and I got you."

"What about yourself, Nadell, huh?" she asked, calling him by his first name. "What are you doing for you right now? Because at the end of the day that is what matters the most."

He shook his head. "Not for me. Nothing matters more to me than getting my people together. That's what I've been out on this earth for. To be a sacrifice for y'all. It's pure and simple. But when you ask me what I am going to do for myself, it's quite clear to me I'm going to continue to fight for you because I love you, and we deserve each other. I'ma give you the space and time you need though. I swear I ain't gon' stand in your way or hold you back from obtaining your goals. I love you too much for that." He stepped to the front door and opened it. "It's supposed to be me and you until the end, Fancii. Just us." He stepped out into the night and closed the door.

Fancii fell to her knees and lowered her chin to her chest. She was so lost and confused. She missed Noodles already. She wanted to apologize to him, to let him know that she loved him just as much as he loved her. She jumped to her feet and ran to the door, pulled it open, and as soon as she did, his car was driving away from the curb with the tires spinning. She rushed back into the house and picked up her cell phone when a text came across the bottom of the screen from Mills. It read: Marsha Brads is a close friend of the family. She liked you two weeks ago. You booked the job. You're going to be a model for Covergirl cosmetics. Call me tonight. I miss you.

Fancii fell to her knees once again. She checked her Facebook and saw that her inbox had two messages from Marsha Brads. One was welcoming her to the team. The other was to invite her to lunch for the following day. Fancii burst into tears. She got to her feet and ran down the hall toward her mother's room. "Mama, Mama, Mama, I got it. I got it. I booked Covergirl. We've made it. Oh my God, I'm so happy!" she screamed.

Angie jumped out of the bed and wrapped her arms around her daughter. "I'm so proud of you, baby. I knew you could do it. I knew you could. I never doubted you for a second, my angel." She had tears in her eyes as well.

Fancii held her mother and cried her eyes out. She was so excited and thankful that she didn't know what to do. "I'm going to get us out if this hell hole, Mama. In fact, I want you to pack your things. We're moving into my condo this coming week." She was over it. Now that she'd booked a modeling job, she needed to get her mother out of the ghetto so she could focus on her career, all the while knowing that her mother was safe and sound.

Angie was confused. "Baby, they bought you a condo already? Wow, those people move fast." She kissed her daughter's cheek. "We're too riled up to go back to sleep.

I'll go put on some tea." She had just stepped into the hallway when the rapid shots started.

Combo and four of his hittas stood in front of Angie's home with fully automatic assault rifles, squeezing their triggers. Boom. Boom. Book. Boom. Boom. Boom. Boom. The windows shattered. Siding exploded in the house. The bullets chopped into the living room. The television fell off of its stand and blew up.

Angie felt the bullets enter into her back one at a time. They felt like flaming arrows, one after the next. They stood her up and turned her around. Her eyes bucked wide open, and then a round pierced her heart. Blood seeped out of her mouth before she fell on her face, lifeless.

The shooting continued. Fancii screamed. "Mama! Mama! Mama, please." She low crawled across the floor as the bullets continued to knock chunks out of the walls. All along the hallway the pictures crashed to the floor and shattered. It sounded to Fancii as if whoever was shooting was never going to run out of bullets. When Fancii made it to Angie, she pulled her into her arms and laid flat on her back with her mother. "Why? Why? Why? Oh my God, why?" she cried, as her pajamas became saturated with Angie's blood.

Combo allowed the last thirty shots of his assault rifle to be emptied into Angie's house. Then he reached on the floor of the van and lit the gas cocktail bomb. He ran ten feet and threw it through the window of her residence before jumping back into the van. "Let's go!" he hollered with a smile on his face under the Jason Voorhees mask. He was ready to turn all the way up. The Game was about to become realer than ever for Noodles and Filipino, he swore.

Chapter 18

A week later was Angie's funeral. It was held at West Angeles Church of God and Christ in Crenshaw. The turnout was only thirty people. Eddie had his men from San Diego on security to thwart any attempts to attack Angie's funeral services. It had been a long week of weeping and trying to figure out who had attacked Filipino's mother and burned her crib to the ground. The community was in an uproar. Because of the event, Noodles had sent Sondra and Cheyenne to a hotel in North Los Angeles. He couldn't take any chances that would allow for anybody to have easy access to his people. He felt like they were being hunted, and he so desperately wished that he knew who the hunter was. Because of the tragedy, Filipino had been popping Percocets left and right and drowning them with Lean. He was taking her murder hard, and Noodles could only imagine the level of pain that he was experiencing.

Noodles gave Filipino a hug and patted him on the back as they stood in the front row of the church. Filipino cried into his shoulder and shook his head in anger. "I'ma find out who did this to my mama, man. I'ma turn this mafuckin' city upside down every day if I have to until I find out who did this shit. That's on everythang, Cuz." He cried a little harder and hugged Noodles tighter.

Noodles returned his affection. "Bruh, I'm riding with you every step of the way. Mafuckas just don't know the wrath they released upon themselves. Angie was my mama too, and I'll handle bidness accordingly."

Filipino nodded. "I know you will, Cuz. Fuck, man. Help me up here so I can see my mother for the last time."

Noodles placed his arm around Filipino's neck, and helped him to walk in front of Angie's casket. Noodles peered into it, and felt sick to his stomach. He couldn't believe that she was gone. She was always so loving and kind to him. He wished he'd stayed the night he'd stormed out on Fancii now. Wished he'd tried to work things out with her in a more appropriate fashion. He was sure that had he been there that Angie would have still been alive.

Filipino felt weak in the knees. He could barely look into his mother's face. She was pale now, her face three times more full than when she was alive. He remembered his last moments with her and he felt his heart ripping in two. His knees got so weak that they buckled. She was his queen. His heart. His everything. She was the only one that could stop him from flying off the deep end. Now that she was gone, he felt that he was seconds away from unraveling. He fell into her casket and broke down. "Aww, Mama. I'ma kill them bitch-ass niggas for what they did to you, Mama. I'ma get to the bottom of this shit. I promise, Queen. I promise with everything that I am as a man." Tears poured out of his eyes.

Noodles was crying too. He hated to see his homie break down like that. Hated to know that they'd lost one of their mothers, an innocent victim in their war of the streets. He tried to pull Filipino out of her casket. "Come on, bruh. I got you. Let's finish the service, let everybody else say their goodbyes, and after we leave, we gon' figure this shit out, Cuz."

Filipino kissed his mother's face. It was ice cold. He laid his cheek against it and closed his eyes. He missed her so much already. His brain could barely comprehend that she was gone. "I love you, Mama. I love you with all of my heart, Goddess. I'ma ride for you. I'ma ride for you until the wheels fall off." He kissed her forehead and allowed Noodles to guide him back to the front pew.

Noodles was doing everything in his power to not glance over to Fancii. Since the attack, she'd refused to speak to him. She didn't return his calls, his texts, and she had him blocked all over social media. He didn't understand how she was taking everything out on him, but it felt to him that she was.

Fancii stepped in front of Angie's casket and looked down on her. She felt like bursting into tears. Her mother was gone. Once again, the ghetto of Crenshaw had stolen another innocent life. This time it had hit so close to home that her family's world had been rocked. She wiped the tears from her face and in the process wound up causing her black sunglasses to become crooked. She fixed them and leaned forward, kissing her mother on the forehead. "I love you, Mama, and I'm going to become successful for you first, and then myself. You were the greatest mother in the world. Please never forget that." She kissed her again. She turned around, walked down the aisle of the church, and out of the doors into the stormy day.

Noodles jumped up and ran down the aisle in pursuit of her. He needed to hear her voice, needed to tell her that he was sorry. He needed to find out how he could console her, how he could be there for her in her time of mourning. But by the time he made it outside, Fancii was getting inside of a black Range Rover. She slammed the door and it stormed away from the curb. He stood dumbfounded. The rain splashed off the top of his head.

Mills reached across the console and took ahold of Fancii's hand. "You okay, baby?" He'd never seen her look so sick in all of his life.

"I just saw my mother for the very last time, so no. I feel like my world has come to an end. I miss her already.

She was my everything." She lowered her face into her hands and broke down crying. "I miss her so much."

Mills swallowed the lump in his throat. He didn't know what to say or what to do. He could only imagine what the loss was doing to her. No one should have to lose their mother by murder. That wasn't fair. From as far as he could tell, Fancii was a good girl. She didn't deserve the things that she was going through. "Fancii, I'm so sorry. I am willing to do whatever it will take to make you feel better, and to help you fight through this. I got your back. Do you hear me?" He rubbed her back and continued to drive.

"Thank you for saying that. To be honest with you, all I ask is that you hold me for the night. I need to cry some of these broken emotions out of me. I'm lost right now. I don't know what to do. I wish I had a way to escape this world for a little while."

A thought crossed Mills's mind. He needed to get Fancii further under his thumb. He needed for her to cling to him, especially since she'd signed a contract with Covergirl that was guaranteed to take her places. He didn't know if that was going to prove to be beneficial, but he felt deep in his soul that it was. There were many ways to get a female under his thumb, but none proved to be more successful than drugs. "You know what, Fancii? When we get to the mansion, I'll give you a few pills to help you relax. We'll cuddle, and you can tell me whatever is on your heart. I'll be there to listen. I promise. That sound good?"

Fancii nodded. "Sounds refreshing." At this juncture, Fancii was willing to do anything that would take her out of the dark realm of pain that she seemed to be stuck inside of. She fully trusted Mills. Unbeknownst to him, she was at his full mercy.

Mills made a left on Western and took it over to Gerald's House of Waffles, where he was set to meet up with Combo so he could drop off his second payment of thirty thousand dollars. So far the thug and his crew had been creating chaos and raising the murder rate daily. The south side of Los Angeles was a dangerous place to be after the sun went down. Fancii's mother's demise was a testament to that. "We got one stop to make then it's all about you, baby. Okay?"

Fancii still wasn't sure if she liked the sound of his names of endearment, but for the moment, she figured she'd roll with the punches. "Okay."

***

At ten o'clock that night, Noodles and Filipino were ushered into Eddie's basement with him leading the way.

"I'm telling you, Cuz, after you niggas holler at li'l homie, y'all gon' get a full understanding as to what's going on. I got four of these fuck niggas down here, but only one willing to talk. I got a whole table full of utensils for you to take your anger out with, Filipino. So handle yo' bidness."

Filipino was hopped up off of three Percocets and a sixteenth of China White. He felt slow and steady. He was high as gas prices during the Fourth of July. He stepped into the basement. It was illuminated by a red light bulb. In the basement were four dudes tied to chairs. Underneath their chairs was a bunch of black plastic. Behind them stood Eddie's crew from San Diego. Filipino mugged each man one by one. He grabbed a hammer off of the table and turned it around in his hand so that the nail extractors faced outward. "Which one of you bitch niggas knows what happened to my mother?" he snapped, already imagining what he was about to do.

Noodles grabbed a saw off of the table and stood at Filipino's side. "Ma'fuckas betta say something or it's about to be a bunch of body parts all over this basement." Noodles was serious. He slid a pair of latex gloves over his hands.

All four men were silent. It was so quiet in the basement that the washing machine was amplified times two. All that were present could hear the dryer as well as it tossed clothes repeatedly in an attempt to dry them.

"Say, Eddie, which one of these niggas you said was willing to talk?" Filipino asked.

Eddie pointed at a small dude that was second from the end on the left. He looked like he couldn't have been older than seventeen. He was skinny, with a blue bandana over his head. "That nigga right there."

Filipino stood in front of him. "So that means that these other three ain't gon' say shit, right?"

Eddie nodded. "I guess so."

"A'ight cool." Filipino raised the hammer over his head and brought it down with all of his might. He slammed it into the head of the dude to the right of the one that Eddie said would talk. He slammed it so hard that it got stuck. Blood poured out of it and ran down the side of his face. He shook in his chair. Filipino yanked the hammer out only to slam it into him again. He picked a random spot on his forehead and busted it wide open. He kicked him in the chest and knocked him over. He straddled him and beat him over and over until nothing but blood and brain matter popped into the air.

Noodles saw what he was doing. "Eddie, hold this nigga right here head back," he said, pointing to the dude to the left of the rat. He started to holler into his duct tape. He begged and pleaded to no avail. His sounds were inaudible, blocked by the duct tape across his mouth.

Eddie pulled his head backward. "Get this fuck nigga, Cuz. That's the only way the Game gon' understand what this shit finna turn into."

Noodles was out of his mind. He placed the ridges of the saw on the dude's throat and pushed down on it before sawing with all of his might. The ridges tore the skin and shredded the muscles and tissues underneath. Tendons popped and became undone. His blood shot into the air only to land on the bags below their feet. Noodles took his anger of seeing Fancii enter into the Range Rover out on the man. His heart hurt. His temper was boiling. He sawed until the blade got caught on his spinal cord. Only then did he stop and fling him to the floor. He stood over the dead body, his saw dripping plasma.

Filipino worked on the next captive. He swung the bloody hammer and smashed in his temple, killing him instantly. He kicked him backward, straddled him, and proceeded to beat his head in for the next five minutes until it was nothing more than mush. At the duration, he stood up, breathing hard. He pointed the bloody hammer at the last captive. "Nigga, you better tell me who did this to my mother. I want answers!"

Noodles ripped the tape off of the boy's mouth. He smacked him as hard as he could. "Did you hear what the fuck he said?"

The boy cried out in pain. "Yeah! Shit! Say look, man, it was that fool Combo and his hittas, man. He did that shit to Filipino's mother. Yours is next on the list, Noodles. He say he gon' make y'all lives a living hell before he ends the both of you. I ain't got shit to do with none of this. I just started rocking with them. I ain't even from Los Angeles. I'm from Sacramento."

Noodles paced back and forth in front of him. He imagined Sondra laying in a casket, or coming to where he'd seen her last, and finding the entire place burned to the ground. This angered him. His mother meant more to him than anything or anybody else in the world. Combo had to pay. He had to feel the wrath for what he did to Filipino's mother. There was no way around that.

Filipino stepped in front of him and mugged him with hatred. "What made that chump wanna target an innocent woman? My mother ain't shit to do with the game. She didn't fuck around in the streets at all. So what type of shit is that?"

The captive did the best he could to shrug his shoulders. "I don't know, man. All I heard was that there was supposed to be a series of attacks against the two of you. Then Combo was saying shit like he was going to drive you niggas nuts before he tortured and got rid of y'all asses. Anybody that's trying to be down with him now gotta swear by that war shit wit' you two niggas or he ain't even letting them come fuck wit' him. Its fifty G's apiece on both of your heads. Y'all don't think mafukckas gon try and fulfill that contract? Yeah, right." He blinked. Blooded dripped from his split lip. The bottom one swelled up like a boxing glove.

Filipino looked over to Noodles. "You hear this shit, Cuz? This fuck nigga waging war on a whole new level. You know what that means then, right?" Filipino's eyes got watery. He was still thinking about the last sights of his mother, and the fact that he and Fancii's relationship had dwindled in every sense their mother had been attacked. She silently blamed him. At least, that was what he felt. It seemed to him that he'd lost a mother and a sister at the same time. Emotionally, it was earth shattering.

Noodles nodded. "Yeah, I heard what he said, Cuz." Noodles stepped in front of him again. "Say, li'l dawg, do you know all of the spots that Combo be at? What kind of security clearance do you have with his crew?"

The dude shook his head. "I'm a low level. He just hired me most recently. That nigga don't talk directly to me. All of the information I get is from the other cats of the crew."

Filipino pulled his 40 Glock from his waistband, pressed it to the dude's forehead, and pulled the trigger twice real quick. He stood back as the dude's brains erupted from the back of his head and splashed against the wall. Then he stood over his form. "Then you's a nobody. That nigga talk way too much anyway."

Noodles scoffed and looked down at all of the slain bodies. He could already tell that it was going to be a bloody summer. The south side of Los Angeles was already turning into a seriously dangerous place to live. Now that there was going to be a war going on, it would only increase the murder rate. It was the life they knew. That's why in Crenshaw if you were blessed to live to see the age of twenty-five, you were considered an O.G. "Bruh, we need to hit Sky up and see what she found out. It's time we clap back at this nigga and hit him where it hurts, before he think it's too sweet. You feel me?"

Filipino replaced his gun. "Yeah, let's do that. She done had more than enough time to do what she had to. We gotta take care of this clown now. I got that murder shit on my mind real heavy." Every time he blinked, he saw flashes of his mother's face. The sight was like daggers to his heart.

"Y'all gon' do what you gotta do. Me and my niggas from San Diego will clean up this mess. We gon' introduce these bodies to the wood chipper." Eddie laughed.

Noodles stepped forward and shook his hand. "I appreciate you, homie. I mean that shit. We gon' get it together, and then all of us is gon' come together so we can claim these streets. The city is ours. One way or another."

Eddie smiled off his true intense hatred for Noodles and shook his hand. He would play his role for as long as he could, just as long as when everything fell down, he was the one that would be granted the pleasure of taking Noodles out of the game in cold blood. He hugged him. "It's all love, Cuz. Let's handle this bidness."

Chapter 19

Sky popped the cork on the Moët, picked up her glass, and poured herself a hefty amount. She set the bottle down and crossed her thick thighs. The purple robe rose enough to show off the underside of her thighs.

Noodles eyed her hungrily. He didn't know what it was about her, but he found her so incredibly sexy. She even smelled good, and for him, a woman's scent was important. "Shawty, what you find out?" he asked, snatching up the bottle and turning it up.

Filipino lowered his head and tooted two hard lines of China White. He was already fucked up after downing a half pint of Hennessy and popping two Percocets. "We need that news, Cuz. That bitch nigga fucked over my mother," he slurred. "We can't have that shit." He rubbed his nose and sat back on the couch with his eyes closed.

Sky shook her head. She'd watched him go through more than a gram of boy already, and he'd only been sitting in her living room for thirty minutes. "I got bitches all throughout his outfit now. They're in his safe houses laid up with his guys. Some are with his security detail. Some are in his traps. You name it, I got 'em placed there. Whatever you need to know, whenever you're trying to hit his ass, I can let you know what's going on inside without a shadow of a doubt."

Noodles drank a nice portion of the liquor. He wiped his mouth with the back of his hand. "That's what the fuck I'm talking about. I knew we could trust you to get shit in order, Sky. I like this shit."

She smiled and sipped from her champagne glass. "Well, that makes me feel good to hear those words come off of your lips. I'm betting that this fool is seeing damn near five hundred grand a day. That's not even counting the work in his trap houses. I'm sure if we added up the street value of all of that, it would push things well over a million. When do we start to hit his spots, and what is the cuts going to be?" Sky wanted to know what she was getting into. She understood that Filipino wanted revenge, but for her, it was all about the money. She had places that she wanted to be in life, and fast cash would get her there sooner rather than later.

"This shit ain't about no money no more, shawty. It's about me seeking justice for my mama. That nigga gotta pay for what he did to her. Me and Noodles already decided on that," Filipino advised her with his eyes still closed.

Sky sat up and placed her drink on the table. "Wait a minute now, Filipino, this isn't what we discussed. Now with all due respect, I understand that you are hurting because of what happened to your mother. I can only imagine the level of pain that you're feeling. You have my deepest condolences for that. But outside of the act of revenge, this is not what we all agreed to before I put my women in place. This was supposed to be about the money above anything else. That's where we need to keep it before it transitions to another place."

Filipino's eyes popped open. His body felt numb. His eyelids were slits. He could barely see out of them. "Bitch, when we hit that lick up in Compton for you, it was just supposed to be about the dispensaries. But then it turned into a job for your locket, and the next thing we knew, we were leaving bodies all over the place because shit spiraled out of control. That's the way the game goes. You'll never know what it's going to be about even a week from today. You gotta roll wit' the punches though. And you gotta crash shit on sight if you ain't trying to be crushed." He staggered on his feet and wiped his mouth again. "Now we can be about the money, but that nigga gotta pay for what he did to my mama. You got that?" He struggled to open his eyes further so he could mug her.

Sky was afraid. She could tell that he wasn't in his right mind. He was fucked up off of the dope and alcohol. Mixing that with grief was a horrible cocktail for destruction. "That's cool, Filipino, just keep in mind that I got bills to pay. My girls are working these niggas as jobs. At the end of the week, I'm going to need to hit their hands with something or else what would make them remain loyal to me, or their tasks? All I'm asking is that you look at things logically."

"What the fuck did you do to that li'l nigga up in Compton?" Filipino snapped.

"Wait, what?" Sky was caught off-guard.

"You heard me, bitch. He kept saying that you weren't innocent. That you knew what you did. So, what the fuck did you do to him?"

Sky waved him off. "I don't know what you're talking about. Maybe you need to sleep that high off. It's fucking you up, Filipino. We need to sit here and get an understanding so we can - "

Filipino rushed her. Grabbed her by the neck, and slammed her against her China cabinet, shattering it. The plates on the inside fell over and broke into multiple different pieces. "Don't play with me, bitch. Do you see smoke in my face? Do it look like I'm joking? Huh? Do it?" He began to choke her as hard as he could.

Noodles stepped beside him. "Filipino, she ain't the enemy, bruh. That fuck nigga Combo is. You're taking your anger out on the wrong person. Let her go."

Filipino continued to choke her. He tightened his grip. A thick vein appeared in his neck. "I'm tired of this shit, Noodles. I'm sick of hutting like this, bruh. Everybody the enemy. Every fucking body except you, man. Even my sister. She hates me too. You wanna take this shit out on me, Fancii, huh? You think I'm the reason they killed Mama. I swear to God I didn't know. I didn't know they were going to do this. So forgive me. Forgive me or bitch, I'll kill you. I'll kill you dead." He stared to dig his nails inside of Sky's neck, breaking the skin, causing it to bleed.

Noodles placed his hands on top of his. "She innocent, bruh. She fucking wit' us the long way. Let this Queen go. She on our side. Please, homie."

Sky kicked her feet. Her eyes were bugged out of her head. She begged for any type of oxygen. Yearned for it. Her caramel face was bright red.

Filipino squeezed harder and they released her. "Damn, man. This shit eating me alive, Noodles."

Sky dropped to the floor with blood running into her robe from the wounds in her neck. "What the fuck?" She coughed, scooting back on her ass.

"I wanna eat tha t nigga, Noodles. I wanna chop that muthafucka into itty bitty pieces and eat him." He fell to his knees and broke down crying.

Sky's eyes were really big now. She stood up. "Look, I'm good. I don't want any parts of none of this shit no more. I can't work under these conditions."

Filipino pulled his gun from the small of his back and aimed it at her. "Bitch, you ain't got a muthafuckin' choice. You understand how short life is. Huh, do you? In one second you can be here, and in the next you'll be a distant memory. Now you riding for the cause, or I'ma blow yo' shit back. You got me!" he hollered.

Sky nodded. "Yes, yes." She backed away with her hands held at chest level. There were a million thoughts running through her mind on how she was going to get rid of him. She already knew that Noodles would also have to bite the bullet, but it was what it was. She feared for her safety with Filipino in the picture. She would report everything back to Combo if she had to. She felt she stood more of a chance of surviving with him in the know than him in the dark. She wished she'd never gotten involved with them.

Noodles stepped in between them. He faced Filipino. "Bruh, she good. She ain't gotta do nothing she don't want to do. Once again, she's not the enemy. Combo is."

Filipino waved them off and headed toward the front door. "You get an understanding wit' her then. I ain't got the patience. We need to find this nigga, Noodles. This shit killing me." He stormed out of the door and slammed it.

Noodles brushed Sky's hair out of her face. "I'm sorry about all of that, Goddess. As you can see, the homie honestly going through some serious shit. We gotta get his head in straight. That's all." He looked into her pretty eyes and continued to toy with her hair.

She knocked his hand away. "That's all. What the hell do you mean that's all, Noodles? Did you not just see what he did to me? Huh?" Tears ran down her cheeks. "He could have killed me."

Noodles sighed and stepped forward, pulling her to his chest. "I'm sorry, Sky. I swear I won't allow for him to hurt you again. We need you. You are very important in all of this." He rubbed her back and tried to calm her down. He wished that Filipino hadn't done what he had. That was going to make things ten times more difficult. Sky already knew way too much information.

"I don't want to no more, Noodles." More tears ran down her cheeks. "Filipino ruined that shit for me. I feel like when he blows, he's going to fuck over everybody, even the ones that are close to him. I can't put myself in that kind of danger. I just can't." She broke out of his embrace. "Let me go. I need for you to leave my house right now. I need to do some thinking."

Noodles shook his head and took ahold of her shoulders. "Shawty, I got you. I ain't finna let shit else happen to you. Trust me, not him. I got this shit."

Sky looked into his eyes for a long time. He was so handsome to her. Even in the distraught and angry state of mind, she couldn't deny his effect on her. She wanted to be close to Noodles, wanted to ride beside him, but Filipino's actions toward her had been enough to shatter the confidence she held in them as a collective team. She smoked weakly. "Hey, Noodles, why don't you give me some time to think about it, okay?"

He exhaled and nodded. He stepped forward and took her small face into his big hands. "That sound good, but don't take too long. I need you beside me. I mean that." He kissed her on the forehead.

She trembled and stepped on to her tippy toes to feel his lips better. "I got you, Noodles. I swear I do." She was trying to figure out a way to get rid of Filipino, and still have the opportunity to get to know Noodles on a fonder basis. He did something to her that she couldn't understand, and she had to have him. If only temporarily.

"That's my girl." He hugged her.

It felt like it was a hundred degrees outside to Filipino. The sun shone bright in the sky. Fancii's suburban block looked deserted. He was ready to go. He was irritated by the Fancii to his very core. He knee that she'd whine something foul to the dude in Compton. He was thirsty to know what it was. Curious to understand who he and Noodles were getting involved with when it came to her. He took the second puff off of the Newport cigarette and pulled out his cell phone. He saw that he had a text from Fancii telling him to call her a-sap. That it was an emergency. That freaked him out. He prayed that nothing was wrong.

He clicked on her number and listened to the phone getting ready to connect their call when Combo and his van full of savages rounded the corner of Sky's block with the side door of the van pulled open. Combo sat on the floor of the van with a Mach Eleven in his hands and a Barack Obama Halloween mask over his face. He saw Filipino from thirty yards.

"Say Cuz, there one of them niggas right here. Pull this ma'fucka up and let's let these bitches ride wit' no mercy. Y'all got that?"

The van sped up, and as soon as they got in front of Filipino, the driver slammed on his brakes.

"Say, potna!" Combo hollered, and then aimed. He had Filipino directly in his line of vision, and then he was pulling the trigger.

To Be Continued...
Street Kings 2
Coming Soon

Submission Guideline

Submit the first three chapters of your completed manuscript to <u>ldpsubmissions@gmail.com</u>, subject line: Your book's title. The manuscript must be in a .doc file and sent as an attachment. Document should be in Times New Roman, double spaced and in size 12 font. Also, provide your synopsis and full contact information. If sending multiple submissions, they must each be in a separate email.

Have a story but no way to send it electronically? You can still submit to LDP/Ca$h Presents. Send in the first three chapters, written or typed, of your completed manuscript to:

**LDP: Submissions Dept
Po Box 870494
Mesquite, Tx 75187**

DO NOT send original manuscript. Must be a duplicate.

Provide your synopsis and a cover letter containing your full contact information.

Thanks for considering LDP and Ca$h Presents.

Coming Soon from Lock Down Publications/Ca$h Presents

BOW DOWN TO MY GANGSTA

By **Ca$h**

TORN BETWEEN TWO

By **Coffee**

BLOOD STAINS OF A SHOTTA **III**

By **Jamaica**

STEADY MOBBIN **III**

By **Marcellus Allen**

BLOOD OF A BOSS **V**

By **Askari**

LOYAL TO THE GAME **IV**

LIFE OF SIN II

By **T.J. & Jelissa**

A DOPEBOY'S PRAYER **II**

By **Eddie "Wolf" Lee**

IF LOVING YOU IS WRONG… **III**

LOVE ME EVEN WHEN IT HURTS **II**

By **Jelissa**

TRUE SAVAGE **VII**

By **Chris Green**

BLAST FOR ME **III**

A BRONX TALE III

DUFFLE BAG CARTEL II

By **Ghost**

ADDICTIED TO THE DRAMA **III**

Hood Rich

By **Jamila Mathis**
LIPSTICK KILLAH **III**
Mimi
WHAT BAD BITCHES DO **III**
A HUSTLER'S DECEIT 3
KILL ZONE **II**
By **Aryanna**
THE COST OF LOYALTY **II**
By **Kweli**
SHE FELL IN LOVE WITH A REAL ONE **II**
By **Tamara Butler**
RENEGADE BOYS **III**
By **Meesha**
CORRUPTED BY A GANGSTA **IV**
By **Destiny Skai**
A GANGSTER'S CODE **III**
By **J-Blunt**
KING OF NEW YORK IV
RISE TO POWER III
By **T.J. Edwards**
GORILLAS IN THE BAY II
De'Kari
THE STREETS ARE CALLING II
Duquie Wilson
KINGPIN KILLAZ III
STREET KINGS 2
Hood Rich

176

STEADY MOBBIN' **III**
Marcellus Allen
SINS OF A HUSTLA II
ASAD
TRIGGADALE II
Elijah R. Freeman
MARRIED TO A BOSS II
By Destiny Skai & Chris Green
KINGS OF THE GAME II
Playa Ray

Available Now
RESTRAINING ORDER **I & II**
By **CA$H & Coffee**
LOVE KNOWS NO BOUNDARIES **I II & III**
By **Coffee**
RAISED AS A GOON I, II, III & IV
BRED BY THE SLUMS I, II, III
BLAST FOR ME I & II
ROTTEN TO THE CORE I III
A BRONX TALE I, II
By **Ghost**
LAY IT DOWN **I & II**
LAST OF A DYING BREED
BLOOD STAINS OF A SHOTTA I & II
By **Jamaica**

LOYAL TO THE GAME

LOYAL TO THE GAME II

LOYAL TO THE GAME III

LIFE OF SIN

By **TJ & Jelissa**

BLOODY COMMAS I & II

SKI MASK CARTEL I II & III

KING OF NEW YORK I II,III

RISE TO POWER I II

By **T.J. Edwards**

IF LOVING HIM IS WRONG…I & II

LOVE ME EVEN WHEN IT HURTS

By **Jelissa**

WHEN THE STREETS CLAP BACK I & II III

By **Jibril Williams**

A DISTINGUISHED THUG STOLE MY HEART I II & III

LOVE SHOULDN'T HURT I II III

RENEGADE BOYS I & II

By **Meesha**

A GANGSTER'S CODE I &, II III

By **J-Blunt**

PUSH IT TO THE LIMIT

By **Bre' Hayes**

BLOOD OF A BOSS **I, II, III & IV**

By **Askari**

THE STREETS BLEED MURDER **I, II & III**

THE HEART OF A GANGSTA I II& III

Street Kings

By **Jerry Jackson**

CUM FOR ME

CUM FOR ME 2

CUM FOR ME 3

CUM FOR ME 4

An **LDP Erotica Collaboration**

BRIDE OF A HUSTLA **I II & II**

THE FETTI GIRLS **I, II& III**

CORRUPTED BY A GANGSTA I, II & III

By **Destiny Skai**

WHEN A GOOD GIRL GOES BAD

By **Adrienne**

A GANGSTER'S REVENGE **I II III & IV**

THE BOSS MAN'S DAUGHTERS

THE BOSS MAN'S DAUGHTERS II

THE BOSSMAN'S DAUGHTERS III

THE BOSSMAN'S DAUGHTERS IV

THE BOSS MAN'S DAUGHTERS **V**

A SAVAGE LOVE **I & II**

BAE BELONGS TO ME

A HUSTLER'S DECEIT I, II, III

WHAT BAD BITCHES DO I, II

By **Aryanna**

A KINGPIN'S AMBITON

A KINGPIN'S AMBITION **II**

I MURDER FOR THE DOUGH

By **Ambitious**

Hood Rich

TRUE SAVAGE

TRUE SAVAGE II

TRUE SAVAGE III

TRUE SAVAGE IV

TRUE SAVAGE V

TRUE SAVAGE VI

By **Chris Green**

A DOPEBOY'S PRAYER

By **Eddie "Wolf" Lee**

THE KING CARTEL **I, II & III**

By **Frank Gresham**

THESE NIGGAS AIN'T LOYAL **I, II & III**

By **Nikki Tee**

GANGSTA SHYT **I II &III**

By **CATO**

THE ULTIMATE BETRAYAL

By **Phoenix**

BOSS'N UP **I , II & III**

By **Royal Nicole**

I LOVE YOU TO DEATH

By Destiny J

I RIDE FOR MY HITTA

I STILL RIDE FOR MY HITTA

By **Misty Holt**

LOVE & CHASIN' PAPER

By **Qay Crockett**

TO DIE IN VAIN

SINS OF A HUSTLA

By **ASAD**

BROOKLYN HUSTLAZ

By **Boogsy Morina**

BROOKLYN ON LOCK I & II

By **Sonovia**

GANGSTA CITY

By **Teddy Duke**

A DRUG KING AND HIS DIAMOND I & II III

A DOPEMAN'S RICHES

HER MAN, MINE'S TOO I, II

CASH MONEY HO'S

By Nicole Goosby

TRAPHOUSE KING **I II & III**

KINGPIN KILLAZ

STREET KINGS

By **Hood Rich**

LIPSTICK KILLAH **I, II**

CRIME OF PASSION I & II

By **Mimi**

STEADY MOBBN' **I, II**

By **Marcellus Allen**

WHO SHOT YA **I, II**

Renta

GORILLAZ IN THE BAY

DE'KARI

TRIGGADALE

Elijah R. Freeman

GOD BLESS THE TRAPPERS I, II, III

THESE SCANDALOUS STREETS I, II, III

FEAR MY GANGSTA I, II, III

THESE STREETS DON'T LOVE NOBODY I, II

BURY ME A G I, II, III, IV, V

A GANGSTA'S EMPIRE I, II, III

Tranay Adams

THE STREETS ARE CALLING

Duquie Wilson

MARRIED TO A BOSS...

By Destiny Skai & Chris Green

KINGS OF THE GAME II

Playa Ray

BOOKS BY LDP'S CEO, CA$H

TRUST IN NO MAN

TRUST IN NO MAN 2

TRUST IN NO MAN 3

BONDED BY BLOOD

SHORTY GOT A THUG

THUGS CRY

THUGS CRY 2

THUGS CRY 3

TRUST NO BITCH

TRUST NO BITCH 2

TRUST NO BITCH 3

TIL MY CASKET DROPS

RESTRAINING ORDER

RESTRAINING ORDER 2

IN LOVE WITH A CONVICT

Coming Soon

BONDED BY BLOOD 2

BOW DOWN TO MY GANGSTA

Hood Rich

www.ingramcontent.com/pod-product-compliance
Lightning Source LLC
Chambersburg PA
CBHW070026260626
47159CB00005B/1965